The Cartel 2:

Tale of the Murda Mamas

The Cartel 2:
Tale of the Murda Mamas

Ashley & JaQuavis

www.urbanbooks.net

Urban Books, LLC
97 N18th Street
Wyandanch, NY 11798

ISBN 13: 978-1-60162-620-2
ISBN 10: 1-60162-620-7

First Mass Market Printing February 2014
First Trade Printing November 2009
Printed in the United States of America

10 9 8 7

Distributed by Kensington Publishing Corp.
Submit Wholesale Orders to:
Kensington Publishing Corp.
C/O Penguin Group (USA) Inc.
Attention: Order Processing
405 Murray Hill Parkway
East Rutherford, NJ 07073-2316
Phone: 1-800-526-0275
Fax: 1-800-227-9604

The Cartel 2:

Tale of the Murda Mamas

Previously in *The Cartel*

Miamor's hands shook as she guided Carter's Range Rover out of the parking lot, and headed for the police station. She had already contacted Carter's lawyer, instructing him to meet her at the precinct. After the Feds searched everyone and took everyone's names, they let the people at the party go.

Miamor kept visualizing the look on Mecca's face when she told him that he poisoned his own flesh and blood. She knew better than to drink anything that Mecca gave her, and she wanted him to feel the hurt that she did when she lost her only sister, so she gave it to Taryn. It might have been coldblooded, but that was the rule of the game: an eye for an eye.

Miamor pulled up to a red light, and without warning, a strong hand covered her mouth. She could smell an intoxicant on the rag that was suffocating her, and she knew it was only a matter of time before her body lost its strength.

She got a glimpse of the man's face when she looked in her rearview mirror. It was Mecca. She was getting weaker by the second. The smell of the strong substance burned her nostrils as she began to slip in and out of consciousness. Trying to struggle against Mecca, she mistakenly put her foot on the gas, and the car began to swerve wildly. "Aghh!" she screamed as she scratched at his arms, forgetting she was driving. Her eyes widened when she felt the car go out of control. It spun wildly and crashed violently against the brick wall on the side of the street, and she couldn't help but think that this was the day she was going to die.

"Hmm!" Miamor moaned as she drowsily opened her eyes and became coherently aware of what was going on around her. "Hmm!" She tried to speak, but something muffled her sounds. She jerked against the chair that she was sitting in . . . she couldn't move. She shook the fuzzy haze from her mind and forced herself to become focused. *Okay. Mia, okay. Stay calm. You can get out of this,* she thought as she began coaching herself. She knew that she had to remain calm, because if she began to panic she would surely die. She was gagged and bound to a chair, her head was pounding from the impact of the crash, and she had no idea where Mecca had taken her. The odds were against her no doubt, and she feared for her life. She knew that she was dealing with a man whose murderous abilities matched her own. Her senses were heightened, causing her anxiety to skyrocket. She bucked against the chair quietly, trying to keep her noise to a minimum. She didn't want Mecca to realize she had awakened. She needed to level the playing field and free herself from her constraints before she faced him. She tried to see through the darkness that had enveloped the room. *Where the fuck am I?* she asked herself. Her body ached all over and she shook uncontrollably as the cold crept through her skin. She smelled the scent of weed burning somewhere in the room, and she realized she wasn't alone. She froze instantly.

Unable to see, her other senses worked overtime as they helped her locate who she assumed to be Mecca. She forced the towel out of her mouth with her tongue and coughed uncontrollably as the pressure eased from her choking chest.

"What the fuck you hiding for, you bitch mu'fucka?" she asked, her teeth chattering. *Why the fuck am I so cold?* She couldn't get control of her reflexes. Her body was shivering involuntarily.

"You talk a lot of shit for a bitch that's tied to a fucking chair," Mecca stated as he stood. He had sat silently in the dark for hours, waiting patiently for Miamor to wake up. She was responsible for the murders of both his mother and sister. He was itching to kill her.

As Mecca flipped the light switch, he appeared before Miamor's eyes. Her vision was blurry. All she saw was a shadow standing in front of her. "What the fuck? I can't see!" she whispered as she shook her head from side to side, trying to clear her vision.

"That's the bleach eating at your eyes, bitch. I'm gon' love killing you. I'ma torture you slow, so get comfortable," Mecca threatened.

Miamor's eyes fell to her thighs. She was naked. Her clothes had been stripped and she had a lot of tiny cuts all over her body. "What the fuck did you do to me?" she yelled.

Mecca didn't respond, but instead he circled around her as if he were preparing to attack. He carried a long thick chain in his hands. It scratched the floor as he walked, making Miamor's skin crawl from the eerie sound. Mecca brought the chain up and swung it with as much force as he could over Miamor's body. A large red welt formed on her thighs where the chain had struck her, cutting her skin almost to the bone.

Miamor cringed in agony as her eyes ran with continuous tears. She was in tremendous pain. She could see the blurry hue of red blood on her legs. Mecca brought the chain down on her again, this time using more force.

"Aghh, f . . . fuck . . . you!" she screamed. She refused to give Mecca the pleasure of crying or begging for her life. For years she had dished out the same cruel and unusual death sentences. If it was her time, she wasn't going to cry like a little bitch, but be a woman about her shit and go out like the killer she was. "Aghh!" The chain whipped her again, this time hitting her bare breasts and stomach.

"You're not gon' beg like your sister, bitch? Huh?" Mecca asked through clenched teeth as he hit Miamor repeatedly. Her bloody body resembled that of a runaway slave, and he found pleasure in bringing so much pain to the person who was responsible for his sister and mother's deaths.

"Fuck you, pussy! Faggot-ass nigga! Fuck . . . aghhh . . . you!" Miamor yelled. Her mind told her to stay strong, but her body rebelled against her.

"Suck my dick, you dirty bitch! I'ma put your ass in the dirt just like I did your sister," Mecca stated. He had beaten Miamor for so long that he was out of breath and sweating furiously. He threw the chain to the ground and retrieved the bottle of ammonia from the corner. He knew that the liquid fire would eat through her skin like acid as soon as it doused her open wounds. He unscrewed the top and splashed the poisonous liquid all over Miamor's bloody body.

"Aghhhhhh!" Her blood-curdling scream was enough to make the average man cringe in regret, but Mecca continued his relentless assault on her without mercy.

Miamor felt like she was burning alive. Her eyes, legs, arms, hell even her hair hurt. She knew that she would never make it out of the basement alive. Mecca had too much to prove. "Thy Father who art in Heaven, hallowed be thy name . . ."

"Who you praying to, bitch?" Mecca asked, taunting her as he slapped the words from Miamor's mouth. "*I* am God."

Miamor could hear the insanity and hate in his voice. She knew that he wasn't going to stop beating her until there was nothing left to beat. She couldn't change that fact. This was her fate. She felt herself growing faint, and regardless of Mecca's taunts, she continued, ". . . Thy kingdom come, thy will be done, on earth as it is in Heaven . . ."

The chain seared through her skin once more, but this time she didn't scream. She was past the point of pain. She was near death. She felt the walls closing in on her. She could see the shadow of the devil standing behind Mecca. She knew she wasn't destined for Heaven. She had too much blood on her hands. She had sinned beyond reproach, and the devil was waiting until she slipped into grace to snatch her soul and damn her to hell. She knew it. She embraced it. She was a bad bitch, and she was going to die like one.

As Mecca's fist collided with her face one more time, she slowly turned her head toward him and spit the blood from her mouth. "Fuck you, Mecca! I hope you enjoy watching me die, just like I enjoyed watching your mother and sister die, mu'fucka!"

"Shut the fuck up!" Mecca yelled, her words chastising him more. He grabbed the ammonia, pinching the sides of her mouth harshly, and poured the chemical down her throat and on her face.

Miamor struggled against his grasp, desperately trying to close her eyes and mouth. It burnt her lips and nose. It was much hotter than any fire she had ever felt. She saw the Grim Reaper stepping closer to her.

"I got something for you, bitch. I'm not gon' kill you. I'ma let my man handle you," he sneered.

Miamor watched as the devil stepped closer to her, and as Mecca walked out of the room. Her heart jumped with each step the devil took. His face came into view, and when it was fully visible, her eyes grew wide in shock. *Fabian!* she thought in disbelief. The shadow in her peripheral vision wasn't the devil, but a part of her wished that it had been. Surely death would have been better than what Fabian had in store for her. He had a score to settle, and she closed her eyes to finish talking with God.

"Give us this day, our daily bread and forgive us our trespasses as we forgive those who trespass against us . . ." Her voice broke, and tears filled her eyes, because she knew that Fabian had the worst intentions for her. He leaned into her, his hot breath blowing against her burning skin.

"It's too late for prayers, bitch. You're gonna die tonight," Fabian stated with no emotion.

Miamor couldn't believe that her past had come back to haunt her. This was the same scary mu'fucka who had begged her for his life just months ago, and now he was standing before her, getting ready to take her life. "I should have cut off your fucking balls when I took your dick, mu'fucka! Do what you got to do, nigga.

Fuck you!" Miamor stated as she regained her composure.

Fabian punched Miamor with so much force that her jaw collapsed on the right side. She felt the weight of her face as her jaw caved in. She cringed, absorbed the pain, recited the Lord's Prayer in her mind, and then spit the teeth and blood onto the floor. She sat up straight and prepared herself for what was in store. She hoped for a quick death, but she knew that it was not going to happen, so she breathed deep, squared her shoulders and forced herself to open her eyes, ignoring the agonizing pain from the chemicals in her eyes. She stared Fabian directly in the eyes and smirked. *This nigga ain't a killer. He'll never be like me. Fuck it! If I'ma go out, it ain't gon' be on my knees.* "Fuck you!"

Prologue

"I'm going to kill you, bitch!" Fabian threatened as he prepared to finish the job that Mecca had started.

Miamor's body was giving up on her. She shook violently from the cold that was settling in. *It's so cold . . . so cold!* she thought as her teeth chattered. Death loomed in the air like an elephant in the room. She could feel death coming. She didn't fear it—unlike the bitch nigga in front of her—she embraced her fate. She smiled slightly, because she knew that she would see Fabian in hell and wouldn't hesitate to get it popping. Even in death, she would be sure she had the last laugh.

She couldn't fight Fabian off of her. She was too weak, and on this day, she felt it in her soul that she was going to die. She knew that she was at a disadvantage. For the first time in her life, she was the weak one. She was at the mercy of the man in front of her, and to make matters worse, she was personally responsible for his strife, so he had something to prove. Miamor knew how niggas thought, and by cutting off his dick, she had robbed him of his manhood. His pride was wounded, and because of that, he would show her no mercy.

The fact that she was a female didn't mean shit to Fabian. He had seen firsthand what she was capable of. He had been her victim, and now she was his. Fate had tipped in his favor, and karma is a bitch . . . a big bitch. He was determined to get his revenge, and it would be sweet . . . slow and sweet.

Miamor was confined to the chair. The ties dug into her skin, rendering her helpless while Fabian attacked her. She felt each blow as he struck her repeatedly. The impact of his fists invaded her brain, terrorizing her existence. Oddly enough, she was grateful for Fabian's attack, because it was much less vicious than the tyranny Mecca had bestowed upon her. Miamor began to laugh slightly because she realized that even at her weakest state she was still stronger than Fabian. Mecca's blows had left her helpless, and made her respect his ruthlessness. Mecca was her equal. His murder game matched her own, but Fabian was beneath her. At this moment, he was physically stronger than she was, but mentally he was pathetic, and she could still sense that he feared her, which is why he hadn't hit her with all his might.

"What the fuck are you laughing at, bitch?" Fabian asked in frustration as he struck her again, enraged that he wasn't making her feel pain like Mecca had.

Miamor had begun to cough up blood, but that didn't stop her from laughing. Her bloodstained teeth agitated Fabian even more as he watched her spit out a glob of blood. She knew that the only way to get out alive was to get inside of Fabian's head. She had to tip the scales in her favor again. She was going to make him fear her without even laying hands on him. He had no heart and she sensed it. She, on the other hand, had the heart of a lion and was about to eat him alive.

Fabian eventually stopped hitting Miamor and staggered away from her. Sweat dripped from his forehead as he looked at her in confusion. His chest was heaving in exhaustion. *This bitch is crazy!* he thought as the dismay he felt spread across his face.

"I let you keep your life last time," Miamor said as she spit blood from her mouth. She was dizzy and she knew that she didn't have much time. Her life was on a countdown. She was slipping away. Her energy was low, and she could feel her life fading. Her body urged her to succumb to the pain, but her mind and strong will pushed her forward. If this was her day to die, then so be it, but she had never given up anything without a fight. She was going to fight for her life, and her weapon of choice was her mind.

"What?" Fabian asked. He was in disbelief at how resistant Miamor was to pain. He didn't know that she was suffering in agony, because she would never allow him to see it.

Miamor was fucking up his mental, playing a game of mental chess where she devised the rules. She could see the hesitation in his eyes. All she had to do was keep talking. "You think my girls don't know where I am right now, Fabian? Even if you do kill me, there are two bitches just like me that are still out there, and they are going to come for you, my nigga," she said.

"Bitch, you can't threaten me," Fabian said nervously as he slapped her once more, the force behind it fading even more.

"I don't make threats, sweetie. I make promises. What? You think they won't know who did this to me? Your fingerprints and DNA are all over this fucking basement, dummy! They're all over *me*, Fabian. We do this for a living. It's not a game with us. We *let* you live last time. You can kill me, but you better know that my girls are gon' come for you, and next time, they are going to do a lot more than leave you dickless. They're coming, Fabian . . ."

Fabian's eyes shifted around the room as if he was the one who was there against his will, as if he was looking for an escape.

Miamor coughed violently and her breathing became labored as she struggled to keep her strength. *Keep talking, Mia. Talk yourself right out of this shit,* she thought. "They're coming, Fabian. Now, you just got to decide. Are they coming to rescue me? Or are they coming to murder you? Killing me won't make you a bigger man. You're stepping into the big leagues by fucking with me, Fabian. Are you ready? Do you think you have what it takes to kill someone like me? Every action has a reaction. Even in death, I can touch you, Fabian. Trust!" she spat.

"Fuck!" Fabian shouted as he began to pace back and forth in the room. He was torn. He didn't want to see the wrath of the Murder Mamas, but at this point, he felt like he was in too deep. He couldn't turn back now. He pointed his gun at Miamor, deciding to just kill her and get it over with. His finger wrapped around the trigger, but when his eyes met hers, he saw the devil in them. His lip began to quiver. He lowered his weapon. "I know you're not just going to let me get away with this. Even if I don't kill you, you're going to come for me."

"Maybe, maybe not," Miamor said. "The point is that you have a chance to live if you *don't* kill me. You show me favor, I might show you mercy. But if you kill me, then you might as well set your watch, nigga, because within the week, you'll be eating hollow points."

Fabian fidgeted, his hand began to shake, and he put his hands over his ears to drown out her words. *"Set your watch, nigga! You'll be eating hollow points within the week."* Miamor's words echoed through his brain, and what had started out as a planned murder was becoming a game of survival of the fittest.

Fabian didn't know it, but he had just transferred the power right back into Miamor's hands by letting her fuck with his psyche. If he had been smart, he would have killed her quick, but he had given her time to think. He had given her the opportunity to bring it to his ass, without even knowing that she had just conquered him mentally. No doubt about it, if Miamor was a nigga, she would have been an American Gangster. She was just that crucial. Even while teetering at the edge of death, she refused to lose.

"I want your word," Fabian said as he pointed the gun back at Miamor. His aim was so shaky that even if he pulled the trigger he would miss his shot. His nerves were shot, and he truly feared the woman in front of him. He knew that whoever made her the way she was had to be ruthless. He hated her, but he didn't want to be the one to bring her death in fear of the repercussions. "If I let you go, you won't come for me. Say it!"

Miamor bit her tongue, because she knew that it wasn't a promise that she could keep, but she extended it anyway in order to save herself. She swallowed what felt like a lump in her throat, but the salty taste of blood let her know that even if Fabian let her go, she could still die. Time was of the essence, and her body was letting her know that if she didn't get help soon, she would be going to meet her maker. She and her sister would be reunited sooner than she thought if she didn't get out of there. "Let me go. You have my word."

Fabian approached her slowly and kept his shaky aim on her as he removed one of her hands from the duct tape. He then backpedaled toward the stairs. Miamor's eyes never left him. They were like a constant threat as he took the stairs upward one by one, until finally he reached the top. Miamor nodded and watched him rush out of the door.

As soon as he disappeared from her sight, she let out a scream of excruciating pain. "Aghh!" she yelled as tears filled her eyes. She used her free hand to try and remove the rest of the tape from her body. Her grip was so weak, which made the effort of freedom so much harder to attain. She was hurt, badly. She could barely breathe, and no matter how hard she tried, she just couldn't free herself from the chair. The world around her spun wildly as if she was on a merry-go-round. In frustration, she rocked the chair back and forth as she struggled to loosen her arms. *Come on! Get the fuck up! Get out of this! You cannot die down here!* she cried silently, forcing herself to move.

Miamor put two hands on the ground and attempted to stand again. She resembled a child who was learning to walk for the first time as she put her arms out to steady her balance. She closed her eyes to stop the spinning and stumbled as quickly as she could up the stairs. She fell repeatedly as blood poured from every opening on her body. Her eyes burned from the chemicals Mecca had doused her with. She could barely see; the world through her eyes was one big blur, making the steps almost impossible to climb. Her bleeding legs, back and arms were unbearable. She didn't care that she was naked; all she wanted to do was get out of there. She needed to get to a hospital quickly. She burst from out of the basement with a desperation she had never known. Panic set in, and her legs threatened to give out. She stumbled out of the abandoned house and onto the city street. She saw people and urged her body to carry her in their direction.

"What the fuck?" she heard someone say. "Oh my God!" another voice called out.

Her vision blurred, and the merry-go-round in her head spun faster and faster as she grasped at the air for support that wasn't there. "H . . . h . . . help me!" she whispered. These were the last words that left her mouth before she collapsed face first. Her head hit the pavement with a sickening thud, causing her entire world to go black as blood flowed onto the streets.

"Help! Somebody help me!" Breeze yelled. She felt the branches and leaves hitting her face and arms like whips as she ran full speed through the thick jungle. She felt the dirt and rocks underneath her bare feet, cutting them and nicking them as she ran, but her only concern was getting away from a crazed Ma'tee. She scrambled desperately, crying to herself as she made her way. She didn't know where she was going. She just wanted to get as far away from Ma'tee as she could. She was going to run as long as her legs allowed her to. She could hear his voice yelling her name, and it only encouraged her to run faster. His voice echoed through the jungles that sat in the secluded Black Mountains, and sent chills through Breezes spine.

She had been locked in his basement for the past eight months, and finally got a chance to escape when Ma'tee had gotten comfortable and let her upstairs. The warm rays of the sun felt unfamiliar to her, because her body had become adjusted to the confinement of the luxury basement that she had been trapped in.

Breeze couldn't see anything but tall, green exotic plants and leaves as she brushed past them with both hands in front of her, pushing them aside to protect her face. She ran and ran until the sound of Matee's voice faded in the distance behind her. She stopped to catch her breath and sat at the base of a tree while looking around in fear. She breathed heavily as tears streamed down her face and her lungs worked in overdrive, desperately searching for more oxygen. The air was thin and muggy, which made it hard to breathe due to the high altitude of the tall mountains.

"Where the fuck am I?" Breeze asked herself as she rested her hand on her chest and felt her heart beating rapidly. Her eyes scanned her surroundings anxiously . . . desperately as she stood back up to continue her escape. Little did she know, she was just wasting her time. The jungle's shape was a gigantic circle, that lead right back to Ma'tee's palace.

While Breeze breathed heavily in attempt to catch her breath, she felt a painful pinch near her ankle. She quickly jerked her leg back and began to examine it, but she didn't see anything. She directed her eyes directly on where the pain was coming from, and noticed a small blood puddle on her ankle that resembled a bite. The sting instantly became an excoriating hurt, and she began to grimace while rubbing the small bite. She tried to stand up, but she quickly was knocked back to her bottom because of her dizziness. Her sight began to blur and sweat beads began to form, eventually trickling down her forehead as she began to experience hot flashes. Before she knew it, she had passed out at the result of all of the pain.

Hours later Ma'tee found Breeze passed out against that same tree, defeat written all over her face. He smiled as he whispered, "Sleeping Beauty," as he approached her. He took his time before

going after her after she had escaped, knowing that
it was impossible for her to navigate her way out of
the jungles. It was nearly impossible for someone to
exit the Black Mountains if they didn't know them
like the back of their hand. Ma'tee approached
Breeze and ran his finger through her hair, hoping
she would wake up. He noticed that she didn't
move and was sweating profusely. She was still
breathing, but something wasn't right. He shook
her with force, but still didn't get a response.

Ma'tee then looked at the exotic tree that she
was lying underneath, and noticed that it was a
black oak tree. He quickly became nervous and
scooped up Breeze into his arms. Her body was
limp, and she wasn't responding to his touch
whatsoever. "See what chu un done to chu self?"
Ma'tee said in his heavy Haitian accent. Ma'tee
noticed the thin red streaks going up Breeze's
legs, an indication of a spider bite. He instantly
knew that she had been bitten by a black widow,
one of the most poisonous spiders found in the
Black Mountains. The black oak was known
for housing their nests. He knew that he had to
get her back to the house before it spread any
further. He had antivenom back home, and knew
it was only a matter of time before the bite would
kill Breeze. He held Breeze securely in his arms
and headed back to his place to administer the
medicine to his beauty queen.

***

Zyir sat in front of the thick glass that separated him and his mentor, Carter. He watched as the guard escorted Carter to the seat. Carter wore an orange jumpsuit, and Zyir noticed that being incarcerated hadn't changed a thing about him. He still had the same confident swagger he possessed the day he went in. He had grown a small beard, but besides that, Carter looked the same.

Carter sat down and looked across at the young man that he had molded into his likeness. Zyir picked up the phone and placed it to his ear. Before picking up the phone, Carter paused and smirked as he looked at Zyir.

"Good to see you, my nigga," Carter said after he finally picked up the phone.

"Good to see you too, Carter. How you holding up?" Zyir asked with sincerity all in his voice.

"I'm good. Ready to see that outside, feel me?" Carter said with intensity in his eyes.

Zyir nodded his head, already knowing what Carter was getting at. "I feel you. I just been waiting for the word, fam," he replied as his adrenaline began to pump.

Their former comrade had turned snitch, and was set to testify against Carter in the upcoming trial, which was set to start a week later. The authorities let Zyir go in aspirations of catching the big fish, which was Carter. The judge had let Zyir out on bail, but held Carter after the DA had informed him of Carter's kingpin status. They saw him as a potential flight risk because of his international drug ties and his unlimited finances, so he was forced to remain behind bars.

"I want you to start putting everything in motion. We un' let them have their time to shine. Now it's my turn," Carter said, referring to the media and the District Attorney's Office. They had made it a big deal in the local and national media that they had captured the head of one of the most treacherous drug rings in the south: The Cartel. They had news conferences displaying the drugs recovered from the bust, and acted as if they had Carter's conviction in the bag, but little did they know.

Carter was just holding his cards for the right time, and since the trial was approaching, it was his turn to make his move. The only thing linking Carter to the drugs was the testimony of Ace. Ace was once Carter's right hand man, but folded under pressure and cooperated with the law; wrong move.

"Everything's taken care of. Mecca is on it now," Zyir said as he slightly grinned.

***

Mecca looked down and watched as his shaft disappeared and reappeared at the expense of Sheila's head game. He placed his hand on the back of her head as he tried his best to stay hard as she pleased him. He was in no way attracted to the girl that was going down on him, but it was all business, and he had to do what he had to do to get his brother, Carter free. He was back in Flint, Michigan, Carter's old hometown, and also the hometown of Ace's snitching ass. Ace was in the custody of the FBI, under the witness protection program, so he had to lure Ace to him, rather than go after a federally protected man.

"I can't believe this shit!" Mecca mumbled under his breath as he looked at the rolls that hung out of Sheila's halter-top. He didn't mind being with a girl with a little meat on her bones, but Sheila was straight up sloppy. She let herself go after Ace got her pregnant, and a couple months after she got knocked up, Ace left for Miami with Carter and Zyir.

Mecca had been dealing with Sheila for over a month and played the role of a man who was falling in love, but in actuality, he couldn't wait until Ace slipped up and contacted her. His time was running out because of the upcoming trial, at which Ace was scheduled to take the stand.

Carter was sure to get life on the drug trafficking charges if convicted.

"I want some of this dick," Sheila seductively said as she rose up and began to slowly take off her clothes.

Mecca stood up with his tool in his hand and watched attentively. He wasn't at all fascinated by her body, but when he saw juices dripping from her pulsating womanhood, he got hard as a missile. His pole grew two inches longer as he stepped out of his pants and slowly stroked himself as she got completely naked. The veins in his rod began to show, and his blood began to flow to his tip. Mecca reached for a condom out of his pants pocket and gave it to her so she could do her trick, which was putting on the rubber without using her hands. He watched and threw his head back and prepared for the ride Sheila was about to take him on. Once Mecca was protected, Sheila straddled him and let him ease into her wetness.

"You like that, Chris?" Sheila asked as she called Mecca by the wrong name.

Mecca almost didn't answer, forgetting that he told her a fake name to conceal his true identity. "Yeah, I like that, ma," Mecca answered just before he took her left breast into his mouth and palmed both of her big cheeks.

Sheila rotated her hips in slow circles while moaning loudly and throwing her head back in pleasure. The sounds of skin smacking echoed throughout the small apartment, which must have awakened the baby, because crying erupted from the next room over, interrupting their sexual flow.

"Ooh shit!" Sheila said as she tried to get as many strokes in as possible before she had to go check on her infant baby boy. "Let me check on my baby," she said as she stopped moving and hopped off of Mecca, leaving him with a stiff one.

Mecca watched as she walked away, and stared at the tattoo that was on her lower back that read "Ace." The thought of Ace made Mecca furious, as he held his rod in his hand.

Just as Sheila got the baby to stop crying and laid him back into his crib, her house phone rang. Mecca looked at the caller ID while alone in the bedroom, and saw that the call was from a blocked number. He quickly sat up and called to Sheila, "Want me to get your phone?" he asked, knowing that Sheila wasn't going to allow that.

Sheila hurried back into the bedroom so that she could pick up the phone. She didn't want Ace to call and find out that she had another nigga in her house. She knew that the money would stop if he knew her little secret. "I got it!" Sheila replied anxiously as she picked up the phone. "Hello."

"Hey, baby," Ace said on the other line in a low calm voice. He was at a payphone in Wyoming right outside of the motel where he was being held until the upcoming trial. He looked around to make sure that the federal agents didn't see him at the pay phone. They weren't supposed to allow him to use the phone at all, but he snuck out while they were asleep to talk to his baby mother. "I miss you," he added.

"I miss you too, baby," Sheila said as she walked out of the room and gave Mecca a signal to be quiet by putting her finger on her full lips. "Where are you at, Ace? I have been worried about you. I haven't heard from you in months," she said as she stood in the kitchen with one hand on her hip.

"I can't tell you that right now, Sheila. But anyway, how my shorty doing?" he asked in concern as he kept looking over his shoulder to check and see if the coast was clear.

"He's fine. He's in there sleep right now. He misses his daddy though. I have been worried sick about you. I can't get a phone call or anything, huh?" Sheila asked with obvious irritation in her voice.

"I'm in some heavy shit right now, but everything is going to be okay in a couple of weeks," Ace said, thinking about how he would start a new life in Wyoming under the witness protection program. He planned on taking his 'hood rat baby mama and settling down so they could raise their son together. He thought that neither Carter nor Zyir knew about his son, but the streets were talking, and it didn't take much for Zyir to find out Ace's little secret. When Zyir found out about the baby, he quickly put Mecca on Sheila.

"I hope so, because we need you here with us," Sheila responded as she smiled at the sound of Ace's voice. She almost forgot that "Chris" was in the back waiting for her to have sex, and she peeked back toward the back of the apartment and saw him opening the refrigerator. She slightly tensed up. She didn't even hear him creeping up behind her while on the phone. She placed her finger on her lips once again to remind him to remain silent. She looked away from him and continued to listen closely to Ace.

"Have you been getting that money I've been sending you?" Ace asked.

"Yeah, I—" Before Sheila could finish her sentence, a loud blast erupted and her brains were all over the kitchen wall. Mecca stood behind her with a smoking gun as he watched her body collapse and the bloody phone fall to the floor.

"Sheila!" Ace yelled as he jumped at the sound of the blast through the phone. "Sheila! What was that?" he yelled into the phone as his eyes began to shift nervously while he gripping the phone tightly.

Mecca let off another round in Sheila's twitching body for good measure, and reached down to pick up the phone. He had been waiting for Ace to call for weeks, and his wish had just been granted. "What's going on, playboy?" Mecca said with enthusiasm as if he was greeting a friend.

"Fuck!" Ace scoffed as he took the phone from his ear and put it on his chest. He already recognized Mecca's voice and his heart rate sped up. He hoped to God that the second gunshot wasn't for his son. He slowly put the phone back to his ear.

"Listen real close, okay? Your bitch is already gone to meet her Maker. Now it's your choice if you want me to send li'l Ace right behind her," Mecca said as he went to the back, set his gun on the dresser and picked up Ace's baby boy. "Hey, li'l man!" Mecca said in a playful voice while still holding the cordless phone to his own ear so Ace could hear him clearly.

Ace sat and listened to the giggles of his own son, and regretted not taking his own flesh and blood out of harm's way. "Don't touch my mu'fuckin son!" he seethed in between his clenched teeth.

"Whoa, whoa! Hold up! You are not in the position to be barking orders, homeboy. You listen to me, and I'ma tell you what *you* are going to do," Mecca commanded as he held li'l Ace in his arm and rocked him gently. "You aren't going to testify against my man. You are going to get up there on that stand and catch amnesia, feel me?"

"Yeah, I hear you. Just leave my kid out of it, man," Ace said in a pleading tone.

"Should of thought about that before you got to singing like a mu'fuckin' bitch. Snitch-ass nigga!" Mecca yelled, getting upset just at the thought of Ace being a rat.

Ace remained silent, knowing that he couldn't possibly snitch on Carter and The Cartel anymore. Too much was on the line. He would rather face federal charges himself than leave his newborn son at the mercy of a nigga like Mecca.

"If Carter gets convicted, say good-bye to your son. It's all on you," Mecca threatened just before he hung up the phone and dropped it. He held Ace's baby up and blew on his stomach playfully, making li'l Ace laugh and squirm. Mecca smiled and hoped that he wouldn't have to send the baby to the same place he had just sent Sheila. He didn't want to be a killer, but snake niggas like Ace left him no choice. He stared down at the baby in his arms and whispered, "It's all up to your daddy, li'l man. It's all up to your snitching-ass pops."

Welcome to The Cartel 2 . . .

The Tale of the Murda Mamas

Chapter One

Miamor

I'm trapped . . . stuck in between my past and my future, and I don't know which one to choose or which way to go. I remember everything that happened to me. It's so vivid in my mind. I can still feel my heart beat rapidly for the love I have for Carter, and at the same time I can feel my temperature rise at the thought of his brother, Mecca. I remember Mecca fucking me up. I can still feel the whip of his chain as it ripped through the flesh on my legs. I can still hear the menacing sound of his voice. How in the fuck he caught me slipping, I don't know, but I can't let him beat me. He can't win, but there's nothing I can do when I can't even open my eyes. No matter how hard I try, I can't seem to wake up. I can't speak, I can't move, I can't do anything, and everything around me is black. I know how I got here, but how the fuck do I get out? For the first time in a long time I'm afraid.

I wish I had my girls with me, because with them, nothing is impossible. With them, we run through niggas like Mecca, collect our paper, and keep it pushing to the next job. But our difference of opinion on The Cartel broke us apart. I did what I thought I would never do. I chose a nigga, Carter, over The Murder Mamas.

I can see the light that so many people talk about before dying, but in my case, it is more like a fire that is waiting to consume me. I'm standing between the gates of hell and my childhood, but they are equal to one another. Either way I go, the pain will be too much for me to handle. My past is something that I don't want to remember. I forgot about it for a reason. I gave myself amnesia so that I wouldn't have to relive it, and I left it behind a long time ago. I don't want to have to repeat it, but I don't want to die either. I have a choice: I can walk into the light right now and let it all end here. I can submit myself to God's mercy and face my judgment in that light, or I can face my past and figure out how my childhood affected me and made me into the woman, the killer, the bitch that I am today. Those are my options; face death or face life. That's a hell of a choice, but I guess it's my destiny. I'm not ready to meet my Maker. I still have too much to do, and there are so many things left in my life unsettled. There are so many debts that I still have to collect on, and so many that I still owe.

So, I'm going to introduce you to my past. I'm going to let you meet the innocent little girl I used to be before the corruption, the money, the bodies, and the bullshit. Don't judge me, just rock with my story as I tell it all . . . the 'hood, the bad and the ugly. This is me, Miamor, the life of a Murder Mama.

Chapter Two

Miamor
1995

Sitting in the bottom of my closet, I shook uncontrollably. The stench of piss was strong in the air, and my hands covered my ears trying to block out the screams. I was terrified. My heart beat uncontrollably and I closed my eyes from fear. I wished I could disappear and avoid the tragedy that was my life, but I couldn't. I relived this nightmare every night.

As soon as my mother left the house, I knew what would take place: The molestation; the screams; the feelings of helplessness. It always happened at the same time. Like clockwork at 1:00 a.m., he came like a thief in the night. No matter how much we avoided it, no matter how many times we begged our mother not to stay the night away from home, nothing ever saved us. She always said no. The bitch made us stay there with him, and even though we cried and pleaded, her answer was always no. If she did not know what was going on, she should have. The shit was happening under her own roof, so I could never give her the benefit of the doubt. Fuck her too! She invited him into her home and unknowingly into her daughters' bed. He was always there, with a fucking grin on his face. We were trapped, and our fates were inevitable.

My sister, Anisa was the victim, and our stepfather, Perry was the bastard who shattered our childhoods. Lollipops and daisies were never a part of our world. All we knew was pain and corruption. It seemed as though abuse and neglect were the only constants in our lives. All we had was each other, and whenever he snatched Anisa from her bed, I always felt her pain.

"Please stop . . . please, it hurts!" Anisa screamed.

Tears stained my cheeks. I could hear my sister crying, but I couldn't do anything. I wished that we could switch places; that was how much I loved her. I knew the pain that she went through, and would take it all for her if I could, but I couldn't. He never chose me. It was always her. She was fourteen, and budding into womanhood early, while I was only twelve and still composed of all elbows and knees. There wasn't a curve to my body, so he ignored me mostly, but he violated Anisa, which meant he violated me.

I could hear the bed creaking from the other room, the headboard banging against the wall as a constant reminder of the atrocity that was happening behind closed doors. We wanted to tell someone, but who would believe us? Perry was smart. He made sure that he never hit Anisa. He never even left a mark. The sucking he did on her premature breasts was done lightly as to not leave any sign of trespass. We were scared, always walking around on eggshells and feeling like strangers in our own house.

The knocking of the headboard against the wall stopped, and I knew that it was finally over.

I waited in the bottom of the closet just as Anisa instructed me to. She always told me to hide and not come out until she came for me. The closet door creaked open and there stood my big sister. Her hair was wild and her eyes were red from crying. I took her hand and led her into the hallway bathroom. I was used to this routine. She never liked to talk afterwards, and she never looked me in the eye. I knew she was ashamed, but what she didn't know was that I was ashamed too, because I just sat there and let it happen to her. I locked the bathroom door and ran a tub full of steaming bathwater. Anisa got right in, ignoring the sting of hot water against her bare skin. She hugged her legs to her chest, and I rubbed her hair gently while we both cried silently as she scrubbed her sins away.

The next day when I awoke, Anisa was already out of her bed. I knew our mother was home because I could hear the sounds of Teena Marie blaring throughout the house. Walking into the bathroom, I saw Anisa leaned over the toilet, gasping for air. "What's wrong, Nis?" I asked.

"Nothing, Miamor. Get out . . . go and get ready for school," she said. She barely got the words out before she was throwing up again.

"I'm going to get Mama," I said. I had never been one of those tattle-telling little kids, but I didn't know what else to do. I could tell from the way Anisa was sprawled all over the toilet that she needed more help than I could offer.

"No!" she yelled, grabbing my arm to stop me from leaving the bathroom. She wiped her mouth with the back of her sleeve and began to cry.

"Anisa, what's wrong?" I asked.

Anisa couldn't stop crying. The deep sob that escaped her lips was a cry that was too mature for such a young girl. The cry signified what she had endured and the things her young eyes had seen before their time. She lifted up her shirt, and I noticed a slight bulge in her belly. It wasn't big at all, but my sister was naturally skinny. Her stomach had always been pancake flat, so the bump seemed out of place on her. I wondered how I could've missed it. I had seen Anisa naked plenty of times, and I had even noticed that she had gained a little bit of weight, but the thought of pregnancy never ever crossed my young mind. I was naïve and green to the game. For months, Perry had been raping my sister, and neither of us ever thought of the possibility of a baby.

"I'm pregnant, Mia!" she cried. "I don't know what to do! I tried to tell him no. He wouldn't stop."

"We have to tell," I said.

"Miamor, no! I don't want anybody to know!" Anisa whispered as she grasped my arm, her teary eyes desperately searching mine as if I could solve this problem. "I have to get rid of it. You have to promise me you won't say a word."

I nodded my head, but tears filled my eyes as I watched Anisa lower her shirt. She was pregnant at fourteen by our mother's husband.

Bam! Bam! Bam! My mother knocked on the door. "I hope y'all ready for school! You better get your asses dressed so you can catch this bus!"

I wanted to open the door and tell my mother everything that we had been through, but Anisa was still gripping my hand. "Don't say anything, okay?"

As badly as I wanted to tell, I couldn't. I trusted my sister and was loyal to her. If she wanted me to keep this secret, then I would. I wiped my eyes, flushed the toilet, and sprayed air freshener in the air before opening the door.

We dressed in silence and headed off to school, our souls heavy and our minds on problems that we were both too young to truly comprehend.

Brooklyn born and raised, we kept to ourselves. It was only Anisa and I. We weren't cliqued up like some of the other bitches in our borough. We had already been jumped on twice behind some beef that Anisa had caught with some girls from her high school, so I learned quickly to stay bladed up. I had seen Anisa put a razor blade in her mouth and carry it around all day without taking it out. I had cut my shit up a couple times trying to be like her, and when they caught us both slipping, she finally taught me how to tuck a blade away in my mouth just in case I ever needed it.

We knew the spots that these girls hung around, and we usually avoided those paths at all costs just to stay out of unnecessary conflict. So when Anisa hit a left and headed up toward their block, I stopped mid-step, not knowing why she would walk right into an ass whooping.

"Nisa, what are you doing? You know if we go that way we're going to have to fight. You're pregnant, Nis. We can't fight them girls off right now," I said.

"I know. I don't want to win the fight, I just want to fight," Anisa said with a determined look in her eyes.

I didn't understand at that moment what she was getting at, but I soon found out. "What?" I asked in confusion, looking at her like she was half stupid.

"Look, I've got to get this baby out of me, Miamor, and I can't tell Mama. I'm too young to go to a doctor and get an abortion by myself. I know this girl who was pregnant, but she got her ass beat and lost her baby. I got to do this, Miamor. This is the only way. You go the safe way. Get on the bus and go to school. I'll see you when you get home," she said. She hugged me and pushed me in the other direction.

Reluctantly, I walked away, confused. My heart kept telling me to go back, but I always listened to Anisa no matter what. I had to roll with her plan. We were both so naïve to think that this homemade method of abortion was the way to go. We had no idea how dangerous it was or the damage that Anisa was doing to her body.

I headed to school, but the thought of my sister fighting alone ate me up inside. After walking four blocks toward the bus stop, I turned around and ran full speed back toward Anisa. It was the first time I had ever disobeyed her. I knew she would be mad, but I couldn't stand the thought of her fighting without me by her side. That's how we were. Where one went, the other one followed, and no matter what she said, I couldn't let her go through this alone. I ran as fast as I could, nearly out of breath when I reached the crowd of girls. I saw the group of girls jumping on Anisa, and surprisingly, she wasn't even trying to fight back. They were stomping her out under the overpass of the train, and my heart ached as I saw them kicking her repeatedly in her stomach and back.

I pulled my blade without thinking twice. They were so focused on Anisa, that they didn't even see me coming. "Bitch!" I brought my blade up and sliced one of the girls across her face, then started throwing mad punches to anybody within arm's reach. Those bitches were twice my size. My little fists didn't do much damage, but with my sneak surprise I had the advantage. As soon as they realized I was there, it was a wrap. It was one of the worst ass whoppings I'd ever taken, but it didn't matter. I was there with Anisa. We took that ass whooping together.

The sound of police sirens blaring caused the group of girls to scatter, leaving Anisa lying on the ground and me kneeling beside her with a bloody lip.

"I told you to go the other way," Anisa groaned as I helped her up. She was lumped up and bruised.

The police officer approached us and hopped into his car. He escorted us home, where our mother threw a fit and sent us to our room. We both sat impatiently looking at each other, waiting naïvely for something to happen.

Hours passed before Anisa doubled over in pain. "I think it's happening, Mia!" she whispered, her face contorted in pain.

"What? What do I do?" I asked.

"Aghh! Miamor, I think something's wrong!" Anisa agonized as she held her lower stomach and crouched down at the side of the bed. A small spot of blood showed through her jeans, but slowly grew to a large stain in between her legs.

"Anisa, what do I do?" I asked. I was panicked. It was the most blood I'd ever seen. It was like her period, but ten times worse, and she was sweating profusely. Her hands were shaking in trepidation.

"I need to go to the bathroom," she said as she took her jeans off and put them in a plastic bag.

I helped her across the hall and locked the door. As soon as she sat down she opened her mouth in pain, but no sound came out. She stood, and blood was dripping between her legs, her thighs stained in crimson. The toilet was filled with it, and it looked like blood clots had fallen out of Anisa.

"What do I do? What do I do?" I asked, my voice cracking from concern and my eyes filling with tears. I knew I was in over my head and I wanted to go run for our mother, but I had promised, and even at such a young age, my word was all I had. I never broke it for anybody.

"I don't know!" she said as she was wracked with more pain. Anisa sat on the toilet as her premature body violently miscarried her baby.

I held her hand tightly as if she was bringing life into the world instead of flushing one down the toilet. I couldn't say anything. It wasn't my decision to make and it was already done, so all I could do was be there for my sister. She didn't ask to be in that situation. Perry had put her in it before her time, so I didn't judge her for wanting to get rid of it secretly.

Anisa was weak and could barely stand, so I helped her to our room and cleaned up the mess.

I gave her two of our mother's pain prescriptions and washed her up before she fell asleep. This was the first time that I was grateful for my mother's ignorance. I didn't want her to come in and find out what we had done.

Just as I went to throw away the bloody towel, my mother was coming up the steps. "Where did all that blood come from?" she asked.

"I . . . um . . . I . . . it was from the fight. I got cut and I had to clean it," I lied.

"Oh, well, that serves you right for fighting in the first place," she said. "I was coming to tell you and your sister that I'm off to work. Perry will be home in about an hour. Come lock the door behind me."

I followed her to the door, and once she was gone, I raced back up to Anisa. She was still asleep. I lay beside her and we wrapped our arms around each other. I knew that we had to get out of that house. Even at such a young age, I was aware of danger. I just felt it in the pit of my stomach that things were never going to get better. With Perry around we would never feel safe, and Anisa had just gone through hell just to hide what he was doing to her. I wanted out. I wanted something better for both me and Anisa, and I promised myself that once we broke free, we would never look back.

***

I awoke when I felt the bed sink down on Anisa's side, but I didn't open my eyes. I already knew it was Perry. I recognized the familiar scent. It made me gag, and I felt a burning at the back of my throat. I hated him for what he had done to Anisa. I knew what he wanted, and I froze out of fear. I lay there stiff as a board, playing possum. I prayed that this night wouldn't be like all the others. It was this night that made me lose faith in God, because if there truly was one, He would have surely intervened. God would have protected us . . . saved us.

"No, stop!" I heard Anisa say. "Please, just not tonight! I can't!" she cried.

I had never heard her sound so weak, and I squeezed my eyes tightly as my heart beat out of my chest. *Please God, help her,* I pleaded. But just like all the other times, God never came.

Perry pulled Anisa by the arm, but I got up and pulled her other arm. "She said no!" I screamed.

Perry stopped and looked at Anisa with a menacing smirk. "It's either you or her." That was the choice he gave her.

I trembled, and Anisa looked back at me while gripping her stomach. I could tell she was still in pain. Tears fell down her face. She hugged me and whispered, "Everything will be all right, Mia.

Go to the closet and wait for me to come and get you."

"No!" I said defiantly, my tears no longer willing to hide. "I'll do it, Anisa. He can take me this time." Snot dripped down my nose as Perry forcefully grabbed me from the bed, carrying me out of the room by my waist kicking, and screaming.

"No! Let her go!" Anisa screamed as she fought him. "Please! Stop it . . . she's too young!"

Perry turned around and backhanded Anisa into the wall and threw me to the ground. "Bitch, get your ass up and let's go!" he yelled at her. I crawled over to Anisa and we huddled in the corner.

"Anisa, don't go!" I whispered.

Perry loomed over us as he unbuckled his pants and pulled out his oversized penis.

"Miamor, go get in the closet," Anisa whispered.

I shook my head no.

"Just do it!" she yelled in between her tears.

Anisa left with Perry, and I climbed into the closet, covering my ears while crying uncontrollably. This had to stop. I couldn't understand why this was happening to my sister. It all seemed so unfair.

"Agghhh!"

The scream sent shivers up and down my spine. I had never heard my sister scream like that. Something was different this time. She needed me.

"Aghh. No! It hurts! Please!"

I thought of all the blood I had seen earlier. All of it had come out of Anisa. I never wanted her to go through that again. I couldn't just sit there and do nothing. I ran out of the closet and into my mother's room.

Anisa was lying there with a pool of blood underneath her while Perry was on top, humping furiously like a dog in heat. It was a sight that petrified me. I thought he was killing her. "Get off of her!" I yelled as I rushed at him and began hitting him. I felt his hand cross my face as he backhanded me to the floor, his wedding ring leaving an imprint in my face.

"Miamor, help me!" Anisa cried.

I ran as fast as I could to the downstairs closet. I knew it was where my mother kept her shotgun. She didn't know that I knew, but I did, and I needed it more than she ever would.

"Mia!"

I closed my eyes at the blood curdling cry. Anisa needed me. I pulled out the double barrel shotgun, but couldn't find the shells as I looked frantically, hands shaking, as I could barely hold up the big gun. Tears clouded my vision as I ran into the kitchen. The headboard was banging loudly against the wall, creating a sickening scene in my head as I pictured Perry molesting Anisa. I tore every drawer out of the cabinets before I sent a box of shells scattering across the floor. My shaky hands barely allowed me to load them into the chamber. I had played with the gun enough to know how to use it with expertise. I was only able to load one shell in. I couldn't waste any more time trying any more than that.

I raced up the stairs and burst into the room. Anisa's hand was outstretched for me as Perry was on top of her. She needed me. Without hesitation, I lifted the shotgun and fired. The blast sent me flying back against the wall.

Perry grabbed his chest as the buckshot filled him. His chest looked like Swiss cheese and he tried to gasp for air.

Anisa jumped out of the bed, blood dripping from her womb down her legs, but before she could reach me, she collapsed. My heart felt as if it was going to burst. I had never been so afraid in my entire life.

I picked up the telephone and dialed 911.

"Hello, nine-one-one Operator. What is your emergency?"

I was out of breath, and I breathed into the phone as I watched Perry's life slip away before my eyes. "He . . . he raped my sister! I shot him! Please, we need help!"

I then crawled over to Anisa and put her head in my lap. "It's going to be okay, Nis. They're coming," I sat in the room with my sister until help arrived. I wouldn't leave her side until she opened her eyes. "I got him, Anisa. He won't hurt us anymore," I said when she finally looked at me. Anisa didn't respond, but from the look in her eyes, I knew that she had heard me.

Once the police arrived and I told them what happened, they handcuffed me and put me in the back of a police car.

I knew that I was in trouble and would probably be going away for a while, but Anisa was safe, and that's all that mattered. I would have done the same thing if I had to do it over again. Nobody could hurt us anymore, and I felt that it was worth it. So, when I went before a judge and told him that I would do the same thing, he said I had no remorse, and was a menace to society. He remanded me to a juvenile facility until my eighteenth birthday. Bitch-ass nigga! After getting the news, I looked at my mother, and she had tears in her eyes, but I knew they were for Perry and not for me. I rolled my eyes at her and then I turned to Anisa and smiled. "I love you Nis!" I mouthed.

"I love you too, Miamor! Thank you!" she mouthed back as sincere tears streamed down her face.

Chapter Three

Miamor

Six years of lockup in juvie was too much to even recall. The loneliness, the abandonment, every day spent there took a little bit more of my sanity away. It was bullshit. Day in and day out it was the exact same. The only thing that kept me going was the fact that Anisa was waiting for me on the outside.

My mother tried to come and see me, but I never accepted her visits. I didn't have shit to say to her because I felt there was no excuse. She wasn't there for Anisa and me when we needed her most, and as a result, I got locked up and Anisa had skeletons in her closet that she would harbor for the rest of her life. I didn't fuck with my mother, and I probably never would. All Anisa and I had was each other. That was enough, and she did my time right along with me, keeping my account full as well as visiting me weekly.

I never regretted my actions . . . not once. That's part of the reason why they made me do all six years. They had me going to therapy as if I needed rehabilitating. All I had to do was show remorse, and they would have let me go early, but remorse for a mu'fucka like Perry was something I couldn't even fake. I hated him. He deserved to die, and the older I got, the more I truly understood that I had done the right thing. Nobody knew the connection I had with my sister. Everyone kept saying that my actions weren't justified because *I* was never actually raped, but fuck everybody who thought that, and fuck you too if you're thinking that! Eventually, my turn would have come, and before it did, I erased that nigga from the map. I did what was necessary, and if the tables were turned, I know Anisa would have done the exact same thing for me.

The day I said good-bye to lockup, I promised myself I would never go back. Doing that much time as a child had turned my heart cold. I had changed, but it wasn't for the better.

Anisa was waiting at the gates. She had really grown up. As I admired her True Religion jeans, matching top and Zanotti pumps, I knew she was doing well. Her hair was cut short in a bob. Her light skin was radiant, and she had the smile of a woman who had seen no struggles. She looked truly happy, as if she was able to let go of what had happened to her. My big sister was beautiful. She was a grown-ass woman now, and I hoped to leave the past behind and be just like her.

I was eighteen, not yet a woman, but definitely not a little girl. I was on my own, and the world was at my feet. All I had to do was conquer it.

"Miamor!" she yelled as we ran toward each other with open arms.

"Hey, bitch!" I replied as we embraced. We hugged and cried in excitement.

"I'm so glad you're out! I missed you, Mia!" Anisa got teary eyed and put her hands on my shoulders so that she could look me in the eye. I already knew what she was about to say. It was something that had been in the air for a long time.

"I'm so sorry, Miamor. I love you. You're my sister. I'm so happy that you did what you did. You saved my life. I'm just so sorry that you had to go through all of this behind my bullshit," Anisa said. "Anything you need, I got you. First thing we got to do is get you out of this bullshit ass jail gear."

I nodded, and we hugged once more before hopping into the car, leaving skid marks behind us as we sped off. She was whipping a nice little Chrysler 300 with leather seats and tinted windows. It wasn't a Benz, but the shit was fly and more expensive than the average whip.

We rode into Brooklyn, and the first place we went was to the salon. My hair was long as hell because I kept it braided while I was locked up. When my shit was freshly permed and wrapped, it was down my back, all natural, no weave. My skin was flawless, and my figure was on point. I made sure to work out daily, keeping myself lean and feminine in the process with curves all in the right places.

After shopping and getting me a completely new wardrobe, we headed to the apartment that Anisa shared with her man, Murder. I was tripping at how freely she spent money. She was cashing out on me like it grew on trees, even giving me five stacks to keep in my pocket until I got on my feet. Her carefree attitude regarding money had me wondering what she did, because I knew her ass wasn't working.

"I can't wait for you to meet Murder. He's really good to me . . . that's my baby!" Anisa bragged as she smiled and batted her eyelashes.

I looked at her in high regard. At first glance, no one would have ever been able to tell what she'd been through. She was the shit, and I admired her for being so strong. I would have thought she would have never been able to trust a nigga. I sure as hell never would. A man who had watched us grow for years had betrayed us without a thought. If *he* could fuck us over, then I didn't put shit past any other nigga out there. Love wasn't in the cards for me.

"What kind of name is Murder?" I asked.

Anisa laughed and replied, "It fits him . . . trust. That's the perfect name for that nigga."

I shrugged as we parked in her building. "You live here?" I asked as we got out of the car. I looked up at the tall sky rise building.

Anisa answered, "Only the high life, babe. I'll put you up on game later. Right now, let's get you settled."

Walking into Anisa's crib, weed smoke invaded my nostrils, lifting me into a contact high almost immediately.

"Babe, come out here!" Anisa yelled.

Murder walked into the room with a blunt hanging from his lips, his aura commanding my attention and respect instantly. Anisa had definitely done well. The nigga was fly. His chocolate complexion and lean figure was attractive. He had a ball player's height, but was a bit on the skinny side. It looked like Anisa weighed more than he did. His face was average, maybe even a little below average, but when I inventoried a man,

I considered more than his looks. The jewels that were hanging around his neck indicated his status, and the fact that he had my sister plushed out in a luxury condo was all the evidence I needed to know that he was getting money. How? I didn't know, but he was definitely papered up. He walked over to Anisa and kissed her cheek with casual nonchalance. He grabbed a couple Heinekens out of the refrigerator and tossed one to me, then handed one to Anisa.

"You must be Miamor. I've heard a lot about you," he said, his strong New Yitty accent complementing his words.

"It's nice to meet you," I replied. "Thanks for letting me stay here."

"Not a problem. You're family. Anisa put me up on everything that happened, and I respect it. You can set yourself up in the extra room." Murder sat down on the couch across from me and passed me the blunt.

Although I had never smoked weed, I accepted it. I had a lot of adjusting to do and a lot to think about as far as my life was concerned, but I didn't want to stress it. I embraced the temporary relief and put the blunt to my lips. I inhaled deeply. Big mistake! My virgin lungs rejected the weed instantly, and I coughed uncontrollably as I put my hand over my mouth trying to hold the cough in.

My shit was on fire, but I was mostly embarrassed, because both Anisa and Murder were cracking up, having a big laugh at my expense.

"You never smoked before?" Anisa asked as the burning finally eased in my chest.

I cut my eyes at her and shook my head no. Her ass knew damn well I hadn't done shit before—fuck, smoke, drive, even flirt with the opposite sex. Hell, I just had gotten out of lockup! I was a virgin to everything . . . green to the game. Everything that the average 'hood chick had experienced by the age of fourteen, I had never been able to do.

"We about to break you in then," Murder stated with a small grin.

Anisa and I sat up all night, catching up on each other's lives, filling Murder in on our childhood and the few good times we had experienced. He didn't interrupt, but instead passed the weed back and forth while letting us do our thing. He just sat back and observed like a gangster would. The weed had me so relaxed and I knew that I had found my new favorite pastime.

By the time daylight crept through the curtains, we were all fucked up. The time had flown by, our reunion making up for the time we were separated. Smoking and drinking all night had me done, but it was the first time that I had felt comfortable in a long time. I was home, and it felt good . . . real good.

***

The ringing of the phone the next morning was like tiny bombs going off inside my head, and when it didn't stop, I figured that Anisa and Murder were just as hungover as I was. Forcing myself to get out of bed, I got up and made my way to the living room. "Hello?" I answered.

Before the caller could respond, Murder appeared behind me and snatched the phone from my hand. He hung it up quickly without even seeing who was calling. "Don't answer the phone, and don't use this phone. I handle business, and business only on this line," he said. His tone was stern, and I wanted to ask him who the fuck he thought he was talking to, but I held my tongue. He was letting me stay at his house and had welcomed me with open arms, so I didn't want to create conflict over something petty. I frowned, but before I could say a word, he went into his pocket and pulled out a wad of money. He peeled off five hundred dollars and held them out for me. "Take this and get a cell phone today. Nobody uses this phone, a'ight?" he said as he softened up his tone. I guess he realized that he had been kind of harsh.

"Yeah, okay," I said reluctantly. *What the fuck is up with that?* I thought as I made my way back to my room. *I know this nigga don't got bitches*

calling here. What else could be so important? I
made a mental note to discuss it with Anisa, and
went back to sleep.

I decided to not even bring the phone thing up
the next day. Anisa seemed happy, and I wasn't
trying to be the one to break up her happy home.
Murder hadn't really shown me shade. I was just
making assumptions, so I swallowed it.

"Hey, sleepy head," Anisa greeted as I walked
into the kitchen. She set a plate of pancakes and
eggs in front of me and kissed the top of my head
as if I was her child, before taking a seat herself.

"Hey, Nis. I'm so fucked up right now," I said
with a half-smile.

"The food will make you feel a little bit better,"
she replied.

"Did Mommy ever try to contact you?" I asked.

"She tried," Anisa said vaguely. She sighed
deeply. "Look, it's like this. I don't have any
family. Family is there for you. They protect you,
and Mommy never did none of that. The only
family I got is you."

"What about Murder?" I questioned curiously.
I wanted to know how deep their bond was. I
never wanted to see Anisa hurt again . . . not by
Murder or anyone else.

"He's good to me. I care about him. He makes
sure I have everything I need. I'm glad he's a part

of my life, but with him, you can't really plan ahead. I have to take it as it is today, because one day he's not going to make it through that door. We both have a clear understanding about where we stand. It works between us because neither of us is looking for love. He doesn't disrespect me with other chicks or nothing, but if it ever came to that, I'm not tripping. He's security, and I need that right now, nothing more, nothing less."

I couldn't really understand why she had Murder on a short term relationship plan, but I didn't question her. She knew him better than I did. In any relationship there is baggage, and she knew what Murder was carrying.

"Can I borrow your car?" I asked.

"You know it, babe," she replied without question.

That was one of the reasons why I loved her so. She wasn't on no fake shit. What she had, she was more than willing to share with me. It had always been that way. If there was only two pieces of bread left, we split it and made ghetto-oneslice sandwiches. If she came across a dollar, then she changed it out and we both had fifty cents. I knew that she would give me her last, and it made me love her even more.

"Where you going?"

"I've got to stop by the mall and pick up a phone. I answered the phone earlier this morning, and Murder kind of flipped," I said.

"Oh, that ain't shit. He only gives that number to people he does business with. Don't worry about it. Even he takes his personal calls on a cell phone. Did he come at you wrong?" she asked, getting defensive.

"No, it wasn't like that. He just let me know not to answer it. He's good. I like him. I think he's cool people," I said, calming her down.

"Well, I'm chilling today. You can call me if you need me. My keys are on the table. Don't crash my shit, Miamor! Your ass probably can't even drive!" she said jokingly.

"Bitch, I got my L's. I took the class in lockup for having good behavior," I answered as I went to dress.

"You? Good behavior? I know you're lying now," Anisa said. "Not one scratch. Mia! I'm not playing!" she warned, her voice following me out of the room.

She knew me all too well, because there wasn't a damn thing legal about me behind a wheel, but I was anxious to spin the block. I just wanted to get out and spread my wings.

Putting on brand new Seven jeans, red stilettos, and a white Ralph Lauren top, I dressed and applied M·A·C cosmetics. I admired myself in the mirror. Everything about me screamed fly, and I knew it. I was only eighteen, so yes, I was arrogant as hell and itching to get into something.

Before I could even hit the door, Anisa stopped me.

"Run them L's, Miamor. I want to see your license before you hop in my car," she said seriously as she sat on the floor in front of the coffee table, rolling a spliff. Murder was stretched out on the couch behind her, his hat dipped low, pistol on his waistline, and flipping the channels on the seventy-two-inch plasma TV.

"Anisa, ain't nobody gon' crash your car. Stop tripping. I'm just going to the mall," I pleaded.

"I'll take her. I'm going that way anyway. I got to pick up a new joint for that job I'm into tonight," Murder said as he stood.

"Fine by me, long as my shit come back in one piece," Anisa said. "I'll teach you how to drive later this week, and take you to handle the official paperwork. The last thing you need is to run into Jake out there with no license. You just got out. I'm just trying to keep you out, sis."

I rolled my eyes. She could tell I had an attitude. Anisa knew she was wrong for sticking me with a babysitter, but I obliged and followed

Murder out of the condo. We didn't talk until we got to the parking lot. He tossed me her keys and gave me a smile.

"I'm driving?" I asked in surprise.

"Fuck I look like, your chauffer?" he asked smoothly as he stepped into the car. "Anisa's your big sister. She's overprotective. I'ma teach you how to drive."

I was geeked and all smiles as I got into Anisa's car. Murder leaned his seat back and put one foot on the dash. "Do you!" he said with a grin.

I turned the ignition and adjusted the seat. Anisa was a little bit taller than me. Once I was comfortable, I put the car in reverse and backed out slowly. My heart was beating out of my chest, only because Anisa's ass had made me nervous.

"Relax, you're good, ma. You control the car, not the other way around," Murder reassured.

I nodded my head, took a deep breath and switched gears to drive before pulling out of the parking lot. Murder was silent as I crept down the streets of New York. Impatient drivers flew past me and I stuck up my middle finger as they drove by, causing Murder to laugh. "What?" I asked as I laughed too.

"Nothing, ma . . . nothing at all. Concentrate on the road. Fuck whoever's behind you," he said.

I put in a CD, and the sounds of R&B filled the car. The music eased some of my apprehension, and I relaxed behind the wheel, as my foot became heavier on the gas pedal. Before you knew it, I was cruising, snapping my fingers to the beat, while Murder rode shotgun, never interrupting my flow. The fact that he trusted my driving made me trust myself, and all of my fears went out of the window. I was whipping through the 'hood like I had been doing it for years. I was on cloud nine as I listened to Keyshia Cole's latest joint. I had never been in a relationship before, so I couldn't relate to the lyrics in the song, but it didn't stop my head from spinning from the feelings homegirl was screaming through the speakers. I couldn't see myself giving my heart to anybody, but I was feeling the song as if my heart had been broken a thousand times. Before I knew it, I was pulling into the mall.

"See, it's easy," Murder stated. He had to be the coolest nigga I'd ever met. He was so laid back, yet his demeanor was so 'hood. "Come on, don't have me in this mu'fucka all day. You can hit up all the shoe shops and shit with Nis. But me and you, we in and out. Cool?"

"Okay," I responded, but in and out became a day full of me tearing up the mall and Murder carrying my bags. I couldn't help it. The little shopping spree that Anisa had given me the day before hadn't quenched my thirst.

Murder wanted to complain, but he didn't. I could tell from the look on his face that shopping wasn't really his thing. He allowed me to shop until I grew tired, and I felt like I had a personal bodyguard with me the way he was mean mugging niggas who were trying to get at me.

"You ready to leave?" I asked. "We've been here all day and you haven't bought one thing."

He sighed and gave me a half smile. "Nah, go ahead. Get whatever you want, ma," he said. "It's on me."

I was like a kid in a candy store, picking up everything that I had neglected to get when I had gone shopping with Anisa. By the time I was done, it was dark outside, and as we walked to the car, Murder asked, "You hungry?"

"I could eat," I responded.

Murder put the bags in the trunk and walked around to the driver's side.

"I'm not driving?" I asked.

He put his hand up and I tossed him the keys. "Nah, I don't got time to coach you through it right now, sis. I got to get to my man before his spot close. Then we'll go grab some food. Call Anisa and see if she's hungry."

I called Anisa, and she declined our invitation to dinner. "I don't feel like getting dressed. Y'all go ahead. Just bring me back something," she said.

I agreed, and then disconnected the call with her. "She said bring her something back," I told Murder.

I reached for the radio to turn it up, but Murder popped my CD out and tossed it in the back seat. "Driver picks the music," he said smugly as he ruffled my hair. I slapped his hand away and laughed as he turned the radio all the way up.

". . . *While I'm watching every nigga watching me closely, My shit is butter . . .*"

Jay-Z's lyrics filled the interior, and no words were spoken, but it was a comfortable vibe between us, and the more I became acquainted with Murder, the more questions I had.

He drove until he pulled up to a pawnshop way out in Queens. I looked around the dark alley we were parked in. A chill went up and down my spine, but I shook the feeling of fear. "Get out," he instructed. He popped the trunk and pulled out a pillowcase, then entered the building from the rear.

When we got inside, an older white man with wire rimmed glasses sat behind a counter. "Who's the girl?" he asked immediately, causing my heart to flutter. The old man shot me a look of suspicion that had me feeling out of place.

"She's good. I vouch for her. She's my li'l sister. Don't worry about her. Let's just handle this business, just like every other time," Murder stated with authority.

"You always come alone," the man insisted, still eyeing me.

I pretended as if I wasn't paying attention, but I was picking up on it all. I was so aware of my surroundings, that the sound of the seconds ticking by on the clock made the hairs on the back of my neck stand up.

"Come on, Schultz, you know me. This ain't a new routine. I don't do bad business, and I'd never bring heat to your establishment. She's with me. She's cool," Murder stated, never showing an ounce of intimidation. He put the pillowcase on the countertop, removed three pistols and then placed two thick wads of money next to them. "I need to make these disappear, and I need another one. An automatic."

The man rose, then locked the front door, flipping the sign to closed. "Follow me," he said.

Murder grabbed my hand and I reluctantly followed him down a long hallway, then down a flight of steps. It was so dark that I couldn't see in front of me, and there was a strong pungent smell in the air. I wanted to cough, but I didn't. My breathing was labored, and I held onto Murder's hand a little tighter for reassurance. *Where the fuck is this nigga taking me? What type of shit he into? Has Anisa ever been here?* I asked myself as a thousand and one questions plagued my mind. I didn't know what I was about to see and when the old man turned on the dim light, and I sighed in relief and released Murder's hand. I felt foolish for letting my imagination run wild. The old basement walls were filled with guns; all types, sizes, and calibers, along with three large barrels that contained some type of liquid.

The man gently placed the three pistols Murder had given him into a metal crate, then slowly lowered them into the barrel. The liquid bubbled and sizzled for a couple minutes before making the guns disappear. He then pointed to the arsenal of weapons behind him and said, "Take your pick. What would you like this time?"

Murder quickly wrapped up his business and led me back out to the alley. Once we were safely back in the car, I turned to him and said, "What was that all about?"

"Don't worry about it, ma. That's not for you. The only reason I let you come inside is because it was dark and I didn't want you in the car for that long. That's the last thing I need is to fuck a nigga up over you in the middle of Queens. You still hungry?"

"Nah, I'm all right. I'm tired now anyway," I lied. I just wanted to get back to Anisa and find out what the fuck was up. She knew exactly what Murder was into, and now I was curious too, but before we got out of the car, Murder grabbed my arm.

"Yo, Miamor," he said.

"Yeah?" I looked back at him and noticed the serious expression he had on his face.

"I know you and Anisa are close and I would never come between that, but I need you to keep what you saw tonight to yourself, a'ight?"

The way he looked at me wasn't menacing or intimidating, but sincere, as if I held his life in my hands. I knew that it was important to him. I had never kept a secret from my sister in my life. She was my other half, and I owed her everything, whereas I owed Murder nothing. But for some strange reason, I nodded my head in agreement.

Chapter Four

Miamor

Months passed, and as Anisa and I grew closer, so did Murder and me. Anisa and I spent day in and day out together. She was my love, and although I wasn't a little girl who followed everything that she did, I still admired her greatly.

Most days we were shopping or taking day trips to the spa. The notion of getting a job was never an option, because Murder made it clear that his lady didn't need a job, and said that since I was just like Anisa, he was claiming me too. So I wasn't to lift a finger. The only thing I did was count his money. The average chick would have been jealous of how close Murder and I had become. I rode shotgun in his car more than Anisa did, but she wasn't tripping because it wasn't like that. Anisa never planned on being with Murder long term. She was just 'riding the wave', she would say. When the ride was over, she was getting off. She would always say that there was no room for love in the life he was living, and since he always said he was never giving it up, they maintained a relationship. They pledged that they would never get too serious. He looked out for her though, and I knew he would do anything for her, because in the short amount of time he'd known me, he gave me his all. He called me his "li'l mama" and kept me grounded, because he said fucking around with Anisa, I was becoming a diva.

All in all, life was good, but I still had no idea exactly what Murder did to fund the lifestyle. All I knew is that when that phone rang, it meant money. Sometimes after answering it, he would be gone for days, but when he'd come back, I'd have a whole lot of new faces to count—big faces—Ben Franklins.

Before I knew it, I had been out for a year, and my birthday was rolling around. Anisa had spoken to Murder about throwing me a party, and although he wasn't really feeling the idea, he consented anyway. I was turning nineteen and feeling myself more than ever. The past year of my life had been amazing, and I couldn't wait to celebrate.

Murder rented out a tri-level loft in Brooklyn and invited the entire 'hood out to the affair. He even paid Young Jeezy to perform.

As I dressed for my big night, I oiled my body down and applied body shimmer before putting on a chocolate Fendi dress with gold braided straps that crisscrossed in the rear, revealing my toned back. My wide hips, flat stomach, and shapely behind had the dress hugging me precisely. My gold stiletto Zanotti's and gold matching clutch were the perfect accessories. The dress was short, and completely opposite of my normal attire. I was usually geared, always fresh with skinny jeans and a cute blouse or top with heels, but that night, I was getting my grown woman on from head to toe, leaving very little to the imagination. My hair was curled and hung down my back, while my makeup was professionally done and gave me a dramatic smoky look.

As I sat on the bed and fastened the ankle strap on my shoe, Anisa walked in. Her strut was runway flawless and her dress effortlessly sexy. "You look like a grown-ass woman, Mia," she complimented with a smile.

"I've been that, you didn't know?" I asked with a smile to match.

Anisa pulled a Tiffany box from behind her back and handed it to me. "Happy birthday, Miamor! I love you!"

I opened it and gasped at the diamond necklace and matching tennis bracelet. "Thank you, Anisa!" I said with a big hug.

Anisa laughed and replied, "I had to give you my gift first. Murder's gift to you is shitting all over mine."

"I highly doubt that." I put the necklace and bracelet on just as Murder knocked on the door. I didn't show it, but I was excited to see what my big bro, Murder had gotten me. I couldn't imagine that anything topping Anisa's gift though.

"It's time to—" he stopped mid-sentence and nodded his head in approval when he saw me, as if my appearance had taken him by surprise. "You look beautiful, sis. Happy birthday!"

"Thanks," I blushed. "Is it time to go?"

He nodded and held out his arm for me. I grabbed it and walked out with him, with Anisa trailing behind us. We were almost out the door when Murder's business line began to ring. He stopped mid-step.

"Murder, come on! Not tonight!" Anisa said, raising her eyebrows in annoyance.

"You're right," he said. He kissed her on the side of the cheek. "It's about Miamor tonight."

I let Anisa walk ahead and I whispered to Murder, "Go 'head and get it. I'll keep her on ice for you," I said, knowing that if Murder didn't answer the call, he would be thinking about the money he had missed for the whole night.

"Cool," he said almost as if he was relieved, and he rushed to the phone and picked it up.

I talked to Anisa on the way down to the car, and told her that he had to go use the restroom to distract her. Moments later, Murder came rushing down the stairs and caught up with us. He winked his eye at me to say thanks, and we got in his car and headed to the party.

We arrived at the club, and the line was out the door. It was ridiculous the amount of people who had come out. Undoubtedly, they weren't all there for me. I didn't fuck with anybody, and I had no friends besides my sister and Murder, but just the fact that the place was packed in my honor pleased me. We stepped out of the limo with a million eyes fixed on us. We bypassed the line and walked straight in, making our way to V.I.P. I felt like a celebrity, and I was all smiles, and so was Anisa.

Murder had an uncomfortable look on his face as he escorted us in. I could tell he was uncomfortable around all the people. His head was on a swivel, and his arm stayed tucked in his hoody, palming his pistol as we entered. That nigga never took a day off! He was always on his toes, and I had to respect it.

The entire place was decorated in turquoise and white. There were already bottles of Cris, Remy Louis XII Grand Cognac, and bottles of Mo spread out in ice buckets around my spot. The music was already at screaming level, and the party was going at full blast.

"If you need anything, let me know. I'ma watch the niggas handling my money at the door and make sure everything goes smoothly. You have a good time. This is all for you," Murder whispered in my ear.

I nodded, and we all sat down to get it cracking.

Murder frequently peeked into the main room and checked on us, and then he would head back to the front door. He didn't mingle at all. Instead, he sat back and watched me and Anisa do our thing.

I was walking through the party, the DJ plugging my name every few minutes making it known that I was the guest of honor. After that, I was shown mad love. Niggas were pinning money to my dress and buying me drinks, regardless of the fact that I had $500 bottles sitting on ice back at the table.

Anisa and I were doing it big, dancing and getting fucked up. I was nineteen and still a virgin, and the slew on fine niggas in the building had my hormones on fire. If I was a different type of chick, I would have had one picked out for the after party, but Anisa had already groomed me. Niggas treated you how you allowed them to, and I was never going to be anybody's a.m. jump off, so I kept my raging emotions at bay.

After circulating the building a couple times, I was about $3,000 richer from all of the birthday money niggas had given me. They were all trying to put their bids in to see who I was going to choose, but little did they know, I was going home alone. I didn't fuck with niggas who paid to play, because a bitch like me wasn't for sale.

I was tipsy, but Anisa was loaded. Niggas was really on her because she had the body of a goddess, and her dress was barely covering her ass. Her dress looked like it was sprayed on, and the bottom of her ass cheeks kept showing as she constantly had to pull down her dress to cover herself. It was all fun and games, until Anisa broke her own rule and became one of the drunken bitches in the club who ended up getting carried out. I noticed her stumble a little.

"Nis, are you okay?" I yelled, trying to be heard over the music.

She shook her head. "I need some air," she admitted.

I grabbed her hand and led her to the front entrance where Murder was. He saw me trying to keep Anisa balanced and rushed over to help me.

"What happened?" he asked.

"She had too much to drink," I explained, while trying to keep her steady. "Maybe we should just go. It's getting late anyway."

Anisa shook her head. "No, Miamor, it's your party. I just need to sleep this off. You stay and have a good time. I can take the limo back home. I'll be fine."

"Are you sure, Anisa? I don't mind coming with you," I replied.

"No, stay. The night isn't over yet," she said.

Murder helped her into the limo and tipped the driver to take her home and make sure she got into the condo safely, then turned his attention back to me. "You good?" he asked.

"I know how to handle my liquor," I said with a smile. "I learned from the best." I was referring to him, because he and I had gotten fucked up together plenty of times since I'd been home.

"Go have a good time. I'll be in shortly. We're closing the doors in a half an hour," he said.

I went back into the club and made my way to my table, but was detoured when I felt someone grab my hand. I turned around to the sexiest nigga I had ever seen in my life. No bullshit. His gray eyes penetrated mine and I smiled. "You're grabbing me like you know me or something," I said with an attitude as I snatched away flirtatiously.

He held my hand up, and I did a sexy half spin so he could admire what I had on.

Drake's latest hit came on, and we began to dance. The dude's hands felt good on my body, and I was beyond intoxicated. Any other day I probably would have smacked the shit out of him, but when my song came on, the liquor told me to make an exception. I was rocking my hips and grinding on him sexily, having a good time, until I felt somebody snatch me up. I looked up to see Murder glaring at the nigga.

"Is there a problem, my nigga?" the dude asked.

"I don't know. Is there?" Murder asked. The look of rage behind Murder's eyes surprised me, and told a story all their own.

The dude stepped back with his hands raised in surrender. "No disrespect, fam. I ain't know she was with you," he muttered. If he did have a chance with me, after seeing him bitch up so easily, he for damn sure didn't have one after that.

Murder snatched my ass all the way across the dance floor and into the back of the loft until we were in a quiet room.

"What the fuck? Murder, why are you tripping?" I asked.

"Don't make me fuck one of these niggas up, Miamor!" he said in an overprotective tone. "Nigga got his hands all over you!" He was yelling, and I had never ever seen him lose his temper. I was speechless. For the first time, I saw a look in his eyes that I had never seen before. I guess I *had* seen it before. It had been there all along, but this was the first time that I had acknowledged it. There was something in the air between us.

"We were dancing, that's it," I whispered. "It wasn't a big deal." We had spent so much time together before, yet this was the first time it felt awkward. My heart was racing and my palms were sweaty. I was nervous around him, not because I was afraid of him, but because I was afraid of the way he had me feeling. I didn't want him to be mad at me or to be disappointed in me. I cared a lot about what Murder thought of me. I left the room and chilled at my table, while Murder hugged the bar until the party was over.

After the entire place cleared out, Murder approached me with the last bottle of champagne in his hands. It had a red ribbon tied around it. "You have a good time?" he asked.

I nodded. "I did. You're too good to me," I said aloud. "I didn't mean to upset you earlier. It was innocent. You acted like I was fucking dude or something."

"I know, Miamor. I over reacted. I don't like the idea of a nigga disrespecting you. I will murder a nigga over you," Murder said sincerely as he looked me in my eyes. "Pop one last bottle with me?" he asked.

I nodded and gave him a half smile as he filled two champagne flutes. He popped the cork, causing champagne to spill over the top. "Happy birthday, Miamor!" he said. "To you!"

"To me!" I agreed as we raised our flutes.

One bottle turned into three as we laughed and conversed with one another. We were both toasted by the time we decided to leave. In my mind, I went over all of the times I had been around Murder. We had formed a bond with one another and it started out innocent, but as I sat across from him, I felt my heart beating furiously inside my chest. The feelings and thoughts I was having were far from right. They were not the feelings that one has for her big brother, but ones that a bitch had for a nigga she was trying to make her man. I was slowly admitting to myself that I was feeling him in a deeper way, and that fact was tearing me up on the inside.

He held out his hand and I followed him out of the loft. My heels echoed off of the concrete floor, and when I got outside, my mouth dropped open at the sight of a silver SL 550 Benz sitting there with a red bow wrapped around it. I turned around and looked at Murder. "This is my car?" I asked.

He smiled charmingly, and I already knew the answer.

"Oh my fucking God!" I yelled as I ran around to the driver's side. The keys were already in the ignition, and I admired the custom leather seats and the wood grain dash. He stood outside, leaning on the back door as I explored every aspect of the car. I jumped out and hugged him tightly.

"Thank you . . . thank you . . . *thank you!*" I screamed excitedly. "This is too much!"

Murder grabbed my hands and intertwined his fingers with mine. Feelings of guilt instantly came back, because we were both letting the liquor cloud our judgment. He kissed my forehead, something that he had done many times before, but my body had never reacted like this. Butterflies fluttered in my stomach, and I felt like I had to throw up, while tiny darts of electricity awakened my southern lips. "Murder!" I whispered as I wrapped my hands around his neck.

"What up?" he asked in a low, raspy slur.

I stood on my tip toes and kissed his lips. I couldn't help it. The voice in the back of my head that was telling me to stop was overpowered by my growing attraction to him. Murder was my brother . . . literally. He was Anisa's man. Even the thought of he and I was wrong, but everything about his touch felt right, like his fingers were made exclusively for me. I was so lost in his embrace. He lifted me, his hands supporting my bottom as I wrapped my virgin legs around his back. I had an itch that I desperately needed scratched. I could smell the alcohol in the air, and I moaned as my head fell back in ecstasy as his tongue molested my neck.

Anisa's face popped into my mind, and almost simultaneously, Murder pulled away from me as if she had invaded his thoughts too. "Wait! Miamor, we can't," he said out of breath. "We can't do this, ma."

I could hear the disappointment in his voice. If we had met in another time or another place, then we would have been so right for each other, but we had not. He belonged to Anisa, and I loved her more than I loved myself. *How could I do this to her?* I thought as I instantly sobered up, the sting of betrayal causing my eyes to burn with tears as I wiped my lips in embarrassment.

"I'm sorry," I said with a hint of sadness in my voice. "It should have never gone this far."

"I know," he agreed as he rubbed the top of his head. We both knew that we had just fucked up. "I know," he repeated.

"How do I tell my sister something like this? She will never forgive me," I whispered. "I'm so stupid."

Murder pulled me close and kissed the top of my head. "Don't worry about it, Mia."

I could not stop the tears from coming down my face. "She's going to hate me!" I cried hysterically.

"Shh! Miamor, Shh! Don't cry, ma. Your sister loves you. I heard about you every day before I ever laid eyes on you. You are all she talks about. She made me love you, Miamor, before I even knew who you were. We both made a big mistake. That's it. She doesn't have to know. I would never break her heart like that. We cannot let this happen again though. It's not meant to be."

It was the first time I had let anyone penetrate my heart, besides Anisa, and I did not like the sacrifice it took to love another person. Love costs too much. I learned on that day that it was sacrificial. In order to obtain it, I would have had to hurt someone else—more specifically

Anisa—and that was something that I refused to do. My sister had endured enough pain in her lifetime. We both had. And although I yearned to know what happiness felt like, I refused to do it at her expense.

As we got into the car, I cried on the inside. This was one more emotional scar that I would have to deal with.

"Miamor?" Murder called as he ruffled my hair playfully. I knew that he was trying to switch the mood back to what it used to be—playful, brotherly and pure—but I moved my head away from him and didn't respond as I stared out of the window the entire ride home. I already told myself that any unnecessary interaction between us would have to stop. I had never been naïve. I knew that things would never go back to the way they used to be.

Chapter Five

Miamor

After my birthday, I avoided Murder at all costs. It wasn't "fuck you" between me and him. I could never hate him, It was more like, out of sight out of mind. As long as I wasn't in his presence, I would never have to deal with what we had done. So, when he was home, I made sure that I was gone, and it seemed like he was avoiding me too. While I used to see him every day, now I was lucky to see him once a week.

Anisa noticed the change in his presence, but she wasn't tripping. He was bringing in more money than a little bit, taking any and all business calls that came through for him, and as long as the paper trail didn't stop, Anisa did not give a damn if he laid next to her at night or not.

Despite our strained relationship, business did not stop, and he still had me count up his paper. He would drop it off on the inside of my door at night while I was asleep. In the morning, I would count it, write the total on a slip of paper and put it all in his safe. It was ridiculous how we were acting, but it was our reality at the time.

Lying in bed, I had not been able to sleep since my birthday. I felt so guilty over what had almost occurred between me and Murder. As I tossed and turned, I knew sleep would not come easy. I threw the covers off of my body and got out of the bed. My head was pounding, so I didn't bother to turn on the lights. I went into the kitchen and poured myself a glass of water.

On my way back to my room, I saw a silhouette sitting in the darkness on the couch. "Anisa?" I called out. I flipped on a light switch and saw her sitting there, anger written all over her face. "Why are you sitting in the dark? It's three o'clock in the morning."

"I'm waiting for Murder to get home," she replied coldly. "That mu'fucka cleared out his safe, and I want to know why. He's barely been here for the past three weeks, and now he moved his money. Ever since I've known him, I've always had access to his paper. He must have met some bitch who got him open, and I'm trying to find out what's up."

I was in shock. It wasn't even like Anisa to be talking like this. "So you think he's cheating?

Anisa, his ass is not cheating on you," I defended him.

"I don't give a fuck about that nigga cheating. He can fuck the entire borough for all I care, but he's not about to be bankrolling the lifestyle of these busted-ass hoes out here. I get the dough. Me, and only me. So when his ass comes through the door, he gon' have to explain to me why I opened up his shit today and the mu'fucka was on E," she said adamantly.

Anisa was livid, and before I could respond, Murder entered the condo.

"Where you been?" Anisa asked him. She got straight to the point, and from the look on Murder's face, I could tell she had caught him off guard.

"Fuck you mean, where I been?" he shot back. "You know what's up."

"Yeah, I do know what's up, and how you been acting lately ain't it. I went into your safe today, and guess what I found?" she asked. Anisa was on a roll because she didn't even give him a chance to answer. Her hands were on her hip and her neck was rolling while her mouth spouted words out like they were on fire. "Nothing, that's what I found. It was empty. Are you fucking with another bitch?"

"Anisa, you're wildin', ma. I don't got time for this shit," he dismissed casually. "I've got business I need to finish taking care of tonight."

"You always got business lately! You never used to hit the streets like this before, and when you were out, the safe was full, not empty! So, you cashing out the next chick now?" she asked.

I could see Murder getting upset, but he was trying to keep his composure. But like every woman does so well, Anisa knew how to push her man's buttons. "Look. I'm not fucking with another bitch, and you know better than to question how I move. I tried to wife you, Anisa. You said you didn't want that. You didn't want to take the risk, talking all that shit about me not being dependable and about you needing a nigga to change before you could commit. Now you in here making a scene in front of li'l mama? What you want me to tell you, Anisa? You know how I get down. Ain't shit changed. It's never been about another bitch. It's about business!" Murder reached into the duffel bag he was carrying and pulled out a thick wad of rubber banded money. "And since it's all about the money, here!" He tossed that shit in Anisa's face, then looked at her in disgust before walking out the door. "I'm out!" The door hit the hinges so hard that it shook the walls.

Anisa threw her hands in the air and screamed in frustration. "Fuck that! I know his ass is up to something!" She grabbed her keys off of the table and looked at me. "Put on your shoes and ride with me for a minute."

"What? Anisa, I'm not even dressed! Where are we going?" I asked, astonished at how far she was taking this.

"We're about to follow his ass," she declared.

I wanted to tell her no, because I knew that Murder was faithful to Anisa. He was never home because of me, but of course I couldn't tell her that. Anisa was tripping over money, making herself look like a real gold digger, and that wasn't even her personality. Murder always took care of home. Whatever reason he had for clearing the safe, I knew it was a good one.

"Come on, Miamor!"

I slipped a hoody on over my camisole and slipped into some skinny jeans. I stepped into my flip flops and was out the door. I had never seen my sister and Murder even disagree, so this full-fledged argument was so out of character for them both. I felt like I was the cause of it. Everything was fine before I made the stupid mistake of kissing Murder.

We slid into Anisa's Chrysler, and just as Murder pulled out of the parking lot, we tailed him, making sure we stayed at least a half block behind him at all times.

"Anisa, are you sure you want to do this?" I asked when I noticed us getting onto the bridge headed out of New York and into Jersey. The look she shot me told me to shut the fuck up and ride, so that's what I did, even though in my gut I knew that something about the entire situation did not feel right.

"You don't know Murder like you think you do, Miamor," Anisa said. "The nigga ain't the saint that he be trying to make himself out to be. You wanna know why you can't answer the phone in the house? The type of business he's into? The nigga is grimy, Miamor."

"He's a hustler, Anisa. He's never done you dirty. How can you say that?" I asked.

"Baby sister, open your eyes. He ain't a hustler. He's the one the hustlers call when they got a problem or when they need to make a problem disappear. He's a killer, Miamor. He would murk yo' ass if the money was good. Why the fuck you think his name is Murder?" Anisa stated harshly as she floored the gas pedal, trying to keep up with Murder.

A killer? I thought incredulously. *I'm around him all the time. How could I have not known? Why didn't he just tell me? I'm a big girl. I could've handled it.*

I was lost in my thoughts and couldn't picture the attentive man I had come to know killing anybody, but then the look of rage that I had witnessed in his eyes the night of my party flashed through my mind. *"I will murder a nigga over you!"* he had said. I could hear his words as if he was in my ear whispering them at that very moment. Syllable by syllable, the phrase replayed in my mind. At the time I thought he was being overprotective, but now I knew that he had meant every word he had spoken. It was something flattering about the fact that he would take a risk like that over me. Instead of feeling fear, I smiled, but quickly wiped it off my face so Anisa wouldn't take notice.

I felt the car jerk as she hit her breaks suddenly, and cut off her headlights. "There that nigga go right there. What the fuck is he doing way out here? He gone make me beat a bitch ass!" Anisa threatened. She was so blind with rage that she was not making sense.

As I looked around, I frowned. We were pulling onto a dead end street. There was nothing around us but old, abandoned buildings. "Anisa, I think you're taking this too far," I finally spoke up.

"I'm not trying to hear all that. All I know is if he's meeting a bitch here, I'm gon' fuck some shit up," she said.

I sighed and noticed lights approaching from behind

"Get down. Here comes somebody," she said.

We inched down in our seats until the car had passed us, and noticed that it was stopping directly next to Murder's vehicle. The brake lights came on, and somebody stepped out of the car. It was hard to see because all of the street lights were busted out in this part of town.

"I can't see shit," Anisa whispered. "Can you see who just got out of the car?"

"I can only see Murder," I replied.

"Fuck this!" Anisa said. She got out of the car and shouted, "Murder, what the fuck is going on?"

"Nigga, you trying to set me up?" I heard a man's voice yell out angrily.

I scrambled to turn on the headlights because I still couldn't see what was going on. Finally, I turned the lights on, illuminating the dead end.

Murder reached for his pistol, but before he could pull it from his waistline, the guy Murder had been meeting withdrew first, pointing a chrome .45 in Murder's face.

"No!" I heard Anisa scream as she ran toward the scene.

"Anisa!" I yelled after her as I got out of the car.

Murder rushed the dude who had to be twice his size, and his sneak attack caused the guy's gun to slide across the concrete.

"Murder!" Anisa cried out as she watched the two men tussle on the ground

Murder finally pulled his gun, but the dude wasn't giving up easily. He grabbed Murder's wrists and used his weight to his advantage as they struggled for power, both knowing that whoever ended up with the steel in their hands at the end was the only one leaving the scene alive.

Anisa ran straight into the confrontation, grabbing the guy by the shirt. He flung her to the ground and muscled the gun away from Murder.

I ran as fast as I could toward them. My flip flops came off halfway there and the gravel dug into the bottom of my feet as I sprinted toward my sister. He had the gun pointed their way, but never saw me coming. I picked up a brick and smashed it against the side of his face with all my might. It was like an ant going against a giant, because although it dazed him, it didn't stop him from firing the gun. He slapped the shit out of me, sending me flying to the ground. I landed on my stomach, something hard digging into my side as I heard the gun shots ring out.

Boom! Boom!

"No!" I screamed. I felt Murder's gun directly underneath me and I grabbed it without thinking, and still lying on the ground, I scrambled backwards and fired.

Boom! Boom! Boom! Boom!

The dude dropped instantly and in the blink of an eye, and behind some beef that I did not even own, I'd caught my second body.

Flashes of Perry came back to me. I started to relive that nightmare all over again . . . Anisa's screams in my ear, the baby she had killed because of him . . . all of the sudden the man lying before me dying was Perry. The dude was scrambling, holding his stomach and choking on his own blood. Shakily, I stood to my feet, walked over to him, and put the gun to his head. I pulled the trigger again and again and again, until the click of an empty chamber forced me to stop, and his blood splatter covered my shirt.

"Oh my God! Oh my God!" Anisa yelled out. "I'm so sorry, Murder! I'm so sorry!"

I could hear sirens in my ears, but I couldn't force myself to move. My feet felt like they were made of cement.

"Miamor, help me . . . he's shot!"

I was in a daze. I heard Anisa calling my name, but it wasn't until I heard Murder call me that I snapped out of it. "Miamor!" he called out sternly. I turned my head, my chest heaving, tears in my eyes, and distress in my heart. "I need you, ma!"

His shirt was soaked in blood, and Anisa helped him to his feet. He cringed in pain as her hands searched his body. "Where are you hit?" she asked, the sirens getting clearer.

Murder lifted his shirt to reveal the vest he wore underneath. "It's just a shoulder wound," he stated. "Come on, we've got to get out of here," he said with urgency.

He led Anisa back to her car and put her in the passenger side. She was crying and kept apologizing over and over. "Get in the car, Anisa!" he yelled as he stuffed her inside and closed the door. He then came over to me. The sounds of the police were right around the corner now. I knew they would be here at any minute.

I looked up at Murder. "I shot him!" I whispered. My hands were shaking. The second murder of my life had not been as easy to commit as the first. This one shook me to the bottom of my soul. *Did he have kids? A wife? He was somebody's son. Did he deserve to die?* All of these things ran through my mind in a split second.

Murder put his hand on the side of my face. "I know what you're feeling, ma."

I couldn't look him in the face.

"Look at me," he said. "You did what you had to do. Now, I need you to get your head together and fast. I need you to get out of here. Take this gun and take care of it for me. Listen to me, Miamor, it's important." He grabbed my shoulders and stared at me intensely. "No weapons, no body, no murder. I need you to make that happen. I'm trusting you, li'l mama. I'll distract the police away from you."

"You're hurt! What about you? He's dead. They'll arrest you," I said as I shook my head.

"Just do it!" He pushed me inside the car and hit the top of the roof. "Drive, Miamor. Go now!"

I skirted out of the dead end and took off down the road as I watched him run back and get into his car. I made a right off of the dead end street just as a police car was pulling onto it. Then, Murder turned recklessly to the left and sideswiped the police car purposefully to get them to follow him.

"Oh my God! Miamor, they're going after him! Why did I do this? This is all my fault! That's not even me, Mia. I don't even do shit like this!" Anisa cried hysterically.

"Shut up, Anisa!" I yelled. "What's done is done. You have to calm down. I have to get rid of this gun, and we need to lay low. I can't think with you in my ear with all that crying."

Anisa sat back in her seat and muffled her cries, while I found myself driving back into the city. I worried about going across the bridge and paying the toll. I was paranoid. If by some chance the police had gotten the plate number on Anisa's car, then they would be waiting for us for sure. If the car got searched, then it would be a wrap, because the murder weapon was under my seat with my prints all over it.

When I came to the toll, I felt like my heart was going to explode. I was sweating, my face was swollen from being slapped to the ground, and I knew I looked a mess. The worker didn't even look my way as she took my money and allowed me to enter New York.

"Where are we going?" Anisa asked.

"I have to do something," I replied quietly. "It's important." I found myself driving to Queens, to the pawnshop that Murder had taken me to when I first got out. I was surprised that I remembered where it was, but instinct led me there. He had told me to get rid of the gun. This is the only way I knew how to.

It was too early for the pawnshop to be open, so we waited. Anisa eventually fell asleep, but I couldn't. Not after everything that had gone down. I was wide awake and more afraid than I had ever been. The moon disappeared as the sun kissed the city streets and welcomed a new day. Hours had passed, and when I finally saw the owner approach the pawnshop, I jumped out of the car and met him at the front door.

"I need your help," I said frantically.

He looked at me curiously, probably wondering what hell I'd been through since my face was bruised and there was still blood all over me. "Murder sent me. I need to get rid of a gun."

The older man nodded and ushered me inside, then locked the door behind us. I put the gun on the counter the same way I had seen Murder do months before.

"It's five hundred each gun," he said.

"I don't have any money," I admitted.

"I'm not running a charity, girl. Five hundred is my price," he stated.

I held the car key to Anisa's whip in my hand. I held it up for him. "Take the car."

"For a five hundred dollar debt you are giving me a brand new car?" the man asked suspiciously.

"Look!" I yelled in desperation. "I need to get rid of this gun. I don't give a fuck about the car. How much is the car worth?"

"I'll give you ten grand for it," the man stated.

"Fine. Give me nine thousand, five hundred dollars and make this gun disappear," I settled.

He nodded, and I followed him to the basement where the barrels of acid were located. After watching the gun dissolve in the acid, I felt relieved.

"You need anything else?" he asked, and motioned toward the wall of guns and weapons.

I nodded. After what I had just done, I didn't want to be caught slipping. I had no idea what type of repercussions would come from my actions, and I wanted to be prepared. "Give me something small."

The old man pulled a small black .25 from the wall. "How does that feel in your hands?" he asked.

I gripped the tiny handgun and nodded my head in approval. "I'll take it."

I rushed out of the shop to find Anisa waiting anxiously in the car.

"Get out," I instructed.

"What do you mean, get out? What's happening?" she looked terrible. Her eyes were bloodshot from crying and she had bags full of worry.

"I sold your car," I said.

"What?" she exclaimed.

"Nis, this car can be traced back to that murder scene. It's not worth it." I split the money I had left with her. "We'll take the subway back home. We need to wait to hear from Murder."

"How did you know where to go to get rid of the gun?" she asked.

I stopped walking and turned toward her. "Murder taught me," I replied.

Chapter Six

Back to the Cartel

Carter sat inside the Diamond Estate . . . his father's home . . . now his home, and sighed in angst from his current circumstance. He had been released from jail just weeks before because the prosecutor's star witness, Ace, suddenly had a change of heart. Carter smiled, knowing that Mecca and Zyir had came through for him and got him off the hook. Now that he was out, he had more important things on his mind instead of prison. Mecca sat across from him, cautiously watching Carter.

Both men were silent, each with a different pain in his heart. The war with the Haitians had been won, but at what cost? They both felt like they had given up too much in order to win. Yes, they still had control of the city, but everything that really mattered in life had been destroyed. Their family had been dismantled all for the sake of power.

"Where is she, fam?" Carter asked aloud as he opened and closed the black velvet ring box that contained the engagement ring that he had planned to give to Miamor. It had been months and he hadn't heard from her. As soon as he was arrested, Miamor had disappeared, and although he could deal with the thought of incarceration and he could handle all of the risks that came with the game, he could not fathom the idea of never seeing her again. He could see her face, her smile, her eyes, as if she had been by his side just yesterday. She was on his brain constantly, and as long as he was unaware of her whereabouts, he would not be able to concentrate on anything else. She was important to him . . . the only thing he had left to keep him sane. She was the woman who was supposed to be his wife and bear his children. *How could she just walk away?* He thought grimly. The thought angered and saddened him at the same time.

Mecca stopped himself from smirking. *Look at this love-sick ass nigga!* he fumed. He was tired of Carter sulking over Miamor. He didn't feel a need to tell Carter of Miamor's deception. He had handled that beef personally, and now that she was out of the picture, he was completely satisfied. He had avenged the deaths of his mother and sister. Although vengeance had come at the expense of Carter's heart, he knew that in time Carter would move on with his life.

"Nigga, you need to take them blinders off when it comes to that bitch," Mecca stated harshly. "She left you stinking. You haven't seen or heard from her since the day you were knocked. She was probably a Fed or something. Forget about her. Grimy-ass bitch was playing a role to get you caught up. You took the bait. It happens to the best of us."

Mecca's words made Carter's heart throb in agonizing pain. The thought of Miamor's betrayal was too heavy a burden for him to carry. "Maybe you're right, bro," he said with doubt.

"Nigga, I am right. That bitch got you around here fucked up. You a clean nigga. She got you growing beards and shit," Mecca joked, making light of the situation. "You need to be thinking about keeping the Feds off your doorstep. Just because that snitch nigga, Ace is in the wind don't mean you're in the clear. The government doesn't lose often. You walking free is an embarrassment to them. They're not done with you yet, so we need to be prepared for whatever they have planned. After your freedom's guaranteed, the rest will fall into place."

Carter nodded, knowing that Mecca was speaking the truth. He was focused on all the wrong things. His life was hanging in the wings, and he needed to be at his best in order to overcome the odds that were stacked against him.

Mecca stood. "I'm outta here, fam. I'll get with you later. I won't be making too many more trips to this side of town coming to check on you. I still got issues left unsettled," he said, reminding Carter of his unfinished business with Emilio Estes.

"Keep a body with you at all times," Carter said with authority. "Don't be on that Superman shit, Mecca. You can't go against the Dominican mafia alone."

Mecca lifted his shirt with one hand, revealing a .380 snub chrome 9 mm, and a .45 tucked against his rock hard abdomen. "Fuck another nigga! I got my bitches lined up right here," Mecca replied arrogantly. "They won't catch me slipping again."

Carter nodded. "I hear you. Be smart and be careful," he said.

Carter arose and walked around the immaculate mansion. The gray sweats and white T-shirt he wore were very uncharacteristic of him. The fear of the unknown had him out of his element, and he spent his days confined to the house, his thoughts of Miamor driving him insane. He had everything in the world that a man could want—power, money, luxury, but without her, it all held no value. He would easily give it all up to be with her, and had thought that her love for him ran just as deep.

Pouring himself a glass of Remy VSOP, he made his way over to the picturesque window that overlooked the front of the estate. A cable van sat on the street, undoubtedly filled with federal agents who were monitoring his home, trying to build a new case on him. He wouldn't give them the ammunition they needed to send him away. Prison wasn't for him. He'd send them to their graves before they shipped him back to prison. He opened the door and walked outside. He acknowledged his armed workers with head nods as he carried the glass of cognac in his hand. Fifty men surrounded the estate, all fully aware of everything and everyone around them, but no one was allowed to enter his home, with the exception of Mecca and Zyir. Carter made his way to the gate and nodded for his keeper to open it. He walked to the edge of the street to retrieve his daily newspaper. A huge picture of his face covered the front page:

Drug Kingpin Carter Jones Walks Free.

The cable truck was not even five feet away from him. He smirked and held up the paper for the Feds to see, then he approached the van. "Good morning, gentlemen," he greeted when he finally reached the driver's side.

"We've been made," he heard an agent whisper from the back. The driver of the van watched him with cold eyes.

"Of course you've been made. Look up and down this street," Carter said. "Cable vans don't quite fit in with hundred thousand dollar cars."

His arrogance and power intimidated even the highest of the law. He could see that he made them nervous. It takes a wolf to catch a wolf. Carter was one man who would not be easy to get to. They were playing out of their league, and their amateur tactics of surveillance proved that.

"Step away from the vehicle, Mr. Jones," the driver commanded.

Carter smiled at the officer's attempt to be dominant, but the tremble in his voice revealed his cowardice. "Not a problem, but I would like to see your badge. Since it's obvious that you'll be guests in front of my home, I need to be sure you are who you say you are . . . you understand," Carter answered sarcastically.

The federal agent removed his badge and handed it to Carter. Carter inspected it with the same hand he held his drink in, then passed it back. He tapped the inside of the driver door. "Agent Marshall," he said as he smiled and walked away. Carter had slyly slipped a transparent audio device, no larger than a small piece of tape, onto the back of the agent's badge, and also one on the inside of the van. *Idiot mu'fuckas!* he thought to himself as he entered back onto his property and disappeared inside his home. They thought that they were watching him, but now he would know exactly what they were saying. He would always be one step ahead of them now that he had infiltrated their operation. The listening device had a radius of 100 miles, and wherever that badge went, Carter's ears would follow. *I'll even hear you fucking your wife at night,* he thought.

Carter rubbed the abundance of hair on his face and thought, *Mecca is right. I need to get my shit together and stay focused.*

Breeze whimpered weakly as a cold sweat drenched her body and chills stiffened her spine. Her light skin was a sickly bluish tint, and she was barely strong enough to lift her head. Ma'tee had tried to stop the poison from spreading, but his home remedies were useless, and the medicine he had given her had no effect on her condition. Breeze's foot was swollen and the skin directly around the spider bite was black.

The red streaks going up her leg was a clear indication that the poison was spreading. If she didn't get medical treatment in a matter of days, she would be dead. "Water!" she whispered desperately as Ma'tee jumped at her every beck and call. The tender way in which he touched her revealed his growing obsession. He was crazy over her. In his mind, no one loved her more than him. He would die before he gave her back. Breeze was the only thing he had left in this world, and he imprisoned her so that she would only be his. She was too beautiful for anyone else to see, too delicate for anyone else to touch. She belonged to him.

He could not see it, but his possession over her was slowly causing her sanity to abandon her. She did not have the strong Diamond will that the rest of her family possessed. Her eyes were empty as if her soul was now gone. She had lost all hope, and as she looked up at the man who had taken her away from everyone she loved, she cried. She didn't have the strength to fight anymore. She was his slave in every sense of the word. He had taken her body, her mind, and her spirit, and trapped them in Haiti. Even if she did ever make it out alive, she would never be the same. Things could never go back to the way they used to be. She had endured too much.

Psychologically, she was ruined. Emotionally, she was drained. Physically, she was raped. The lovely young woman that Breeze used to be did not exist anymore. Only Ma'tee had the key to set her free, and she knew that would never happen.

Breeze began to cough violently and bile flew from her mouth, her body desperately trying to get rid of some of the venom that was slowly killing her.

Ma'tee sat near her bedside and applied ice to her wound and a cold wet towel to her forehead to try and lower her fever. Her temperature was dangerously high, yet she felt so cold that she shivered. He desperately tried to bring Breeze's health back up to par, but the more days that passed, the worse she became. He wasn't ready to let her go. He refused to lose her, even to death, so his only alternative was to take her to the only doctor in town. Ma'tee knew that he was taking a big risk by taking Breeze to town, but if he wanted her to live, then he had to.

He stood to his feet and looked around at all of the Polaroid pictures he had taken of Breeze. They covered the walls, almost entirely constructing his very own wallpaper of lunacy. They were his masterpiece. "So beautiful!" he whispered. The photos chronicled her time in Haiti. Her smileless face and hateful expressions went unnoticed by him. He was delirious to think that he loved her. The misery and fear that he was causing her was evident on her face in every photograph. He went upstairs to retrieve his gun, rummaging through his kitchen drawers until he found bullets to load it with. He was unsure about taking her to town, but his hand was forced. He did not have a choice.

Ma'tee returned to her side. "Me princess," he said as he stroked her face with the nose of his gun.

Breeze turned her head in disgust, causing her to vomit even more.

"Me am going to take you to town to see de medical doctor, but chu have to promise not to run. Me run de entire city. If chu say one word to anybody, me will kill chu, young Breeze. Chu understand?"

Breeze did not respond. Hot tears had dried on her ashen face.

"Do chu understand?" Ma'tee asked again.

Breeze nodded her head and felt Ma'tee lift her from the bed. The feel of his hands on her body made her cringe as he carried her to the back of his mansion and into the thick of the jungle. The average person would become lost in the jungle-filled mountain terrain, but Ma'tee had grown up here. He navigated the area well, and knew the dangers that lay underneath the deceiving appearance of the land. Even the most beautiful flower could be deadly.

Breeze tried her hardest to remember the path that Ma'tee took, so that she would know the way to town, but she was so weak and everything looked the same.

"Chu will never remember de way," he said as if he was reading her mind. "So stop trying."

They came to a clearing where a green Hummer sat covered in a tarp that was disguised by brush and leaves. Ma'tee sat Breeze down on the ground and removed the large tarp, then placed her in the passenger seat.

There's a car here, she thought. *I have to remember how to get back to this spot,* she told herself.

Ma'tee started the Hummer and rode the rough terrain the rest of the way down the mountain, navigating the deadly path like an expert, until he reached the town below.

For the first time in months, Breeze saw other faces besides Ma'tee's as they passed some of the townspeople, but her health was fading. Everything appeared blurry, and the pain radiating through her body was becoming unbearable.

Ma'tee drove with one hand on his gun and the other on his steering wheel. "Remember what me told chu," he instructed as the car finally stopped moving.

He attempted to carry her out of the car, but she fought him, pushing him off of her. "Don't touch me! I'll walk!" she screamed in frustration. She shook like a leaf in a strong wind as she stepped out of the car, but she was determined to not have his hands on her in public. However, when she put weight onto her poisoned foot, her body came crashing down like a house of cards.

"Stop fighting me and let me help chu," Ma'tee whispered the words, but it sounded more like a demand as he bent down and scooped her up in his arms.

She had lost a considerable amount of weight and was light as a feather. Against her will, her head fell onto his chest and she looked up at her captor. It was the first time she had ever looked directly at Ma'tee, and his heart melted into her grey eyes. "Please, let me go!" she pleaded.

"I can never do that, my princess. Once you learn to love me, your life will be filled with riches," he promised. He carried her into the doctor's office and rushed over to the receptionist's desk. "Please, help me! Me daughter was bitten by a black widow and is extremely sick!"

The receptionist took one look at Breeze and stood to her feet in a panic. "Doctor!"

The most beautiful woman Breeze had ever seen came rushing out of the back. "Oh my!" she exclaimed at Breeze's condition. "Please, put her over here . . . hurry!" Ma'tee rushed and placed Breeze on a stretcher. The doctor began to wheel her to the back of the office while Ma'tee followed closely behind.

"No, please sir, chu need to wait up front and let me do me job. Me will take care of she," the doctor reassured. "Me receptionist has paperwork for chu to fill out. Me will keep chu updated."

Ma'tee's eyes shifted from the doctor to Breeze as he became nervous. He had not planned on leaving Breeze's side. He nodded and said, "Can I just speak to me daughter for one moment?"

The doctor nodded and Ma'tee walked over to Breeze. "Me will kill chu!" he said as he wrapped his hands around her tiny neck. He applied pressure and leaned over her so that the doctor could not see what he was doing. He had killed many men in his lifetime, and he knew that there was a delicate balance between death and unconsciousness.

Breeze felt her oxygen being cut off, and she wanted to struggle, but her body felt so heavy. The poison was rendering her helpless.

"If chu say a word, me will kill chu."

Those were the last words she heard before she went unconscious. Ma'tee had cut off her air supply long enough to knock her out without killing her. He hoped she would stay that way until the doctor would allow him to be by her side again. He turned to the doctor in panic. "She's passed out! Please help she!" he whispered as he wiped tears from his eyes.

"It's de poison. It's shutting down her nervous system. Why didn't chu get help sooner?" the doctor asked.

Ma'tee played the grieving father well. He acted as if he was so choked up that he couldn't respond.

"Me will do all me can," the doctor said before taking Breeze and disappearing behind two double doors.

Ma'tee paced back and forth in the waiting area for two hours. He kept watching the clock, each minute taunting him and threatening to expose him. Finally, the doctor emerged through the double doors.

"How is she?" Ma'tee asked.

"She will be fine, with medicine and rest," the doctor replied.

"Can me see her?" he asked.

The doctor shook her head. "Not right now. She is still asleep. We have her in a sterile recovery room. Me cannot allow chu back there and risk infection. When she awakens, me will come get chu."

Ma'tee sat down impatiently, his leg bouncing in anticipation as he watched the doctor disappear into the back once more.

Breeze's eyes were so heavy that she could barely open them. Flashes of white light sneaked through her closed lids as she slowly came out of the anesthesia. Her head was groggy, and she could barely remember where she was, but when she closed her eyes, it all came rushing back to her like a bad dream: The jungle; the spider bite; the doctor. Every detail was fuzzy, but it was all slowly coming back to her. *I'm at the doctor's office. I have to get out of here before Ma'tee comes for me,* she thought. It took all of her might to roll onto her side. Her neck felt as if she were a newborn baby. She couldn't support her head and her vision was blurry. *Get up!* she urged herself. *Get up!* There was an IV in her arm. She snatched at it. She was so weak that she could barely get the needle out of her arm. Forcing herself to sit up, she stood on wobbly legs which caused excruciating pain to shoot up the right side of her body. She shook her head from side to side trying to clear her vision, and saw that she had an incision that ran down the length of her leg, and that her foot was bandaged. The anesthetic hadn't completely worn, off and it was hard for her to stay focused. Her limbs were so lazy, every move she made exhausted her, but she fought the urge to lie back down.

The ringing of a phone snapped her to attention. *I have to get to that phone,* she thought. Breeze was in a state of emergency. This was her only shot to reach out to her family. She knew that if she didn't make it to that phone, she could kiss everything she ever knew good-bye.

She forced herself to stand on her injured foot. She wanted to scream at the pain that she felt when she was fully standing, but instead, she closed her eyes and took deep breaths until the blinding ache died down and she was able to move. The excruciation kept her alert as she used the objects in the room to help her toward the door. "Where is the phone?" she whispered to herself. She stuck her head into the hallway. She could see the double doors that led to the lobby. Behind them was Ma'tee, lurking, preying on her. Her heart rate increased from the fear of seeing his face again.

Desperation and adrenaline filled her as she put her back against the wall and crept to the next room. She opened the door and frantically scanned for a phone. "Thank you, God!" she cried as she rushed toward it. Moving too quickly, she fell. "Aghh!" she accidentally cried out as her leg hit the floor. She covered her mouth to stop herself from making too much noise. Tears flooded her face as she reached for the phone. The dial tone she heard was like music to her ears. Her fingers trembled as she tried to dial out, causing her to call the wrong number, 810. *Shit! What is his number?* Her mind was so frantic that she could barely recall the correct sequence, 1-810-625-1816.

She could hear footsteps coming down the hallway, and she cradled the phone for dear life. *Please answer! Come on, please pick up!*

Ring! Ring!

Answer! she begged as the footsteps drew closer.

Please, I need you . . .

Ring! Ring!

Zyir bobbed his head to the Rick Ross that was blaring from his speakers, when he felt his cell phone vibrate on his hip. He was on his way back from Opa-locka, and he had a quarter million dollars in his trunk and rode with a pistol in his lap for extra security. He turned down the stereo and looked at the unknown call coming in on his BlackBerry. "Yo?" he answered.

All he heard was crying in the phone, and he started to end the call thinking that someone had the wrong number.

"Zy . . . Zyir!" the shaky voice said.

He recognized her voice instantly. Emotions came rushing over him. "Breeze?" he whispered in disbelief as his heart sank into his stomach.

Breeze was so hysterical when she heard him answer the phone that she couldn't get her words together. Every time she tried to speak, only sobs came out.

"Breeze, talk to me, ma! Calm down! Where are you? You've got to tell me where you are!" she heard him yell.

Just the sound of his voice caused her to fall apart. "Zyir!" she whispered frantically. "Zyir, please . . ." were the only words she was able to get out before the footsteps were at the door. She hurried and pushed the telephone underneath the bed, but didn't disconnect the call.

The door opened, and a confused doctor rushed inside. "What are chu doing in here? Chu should still be in recovery," she said.

"Please, Zyir . . . I have to talk to Zyir!" Breeze pleaded with the doctor, but she was quickly silenced when she heard Ma'tee demanding to see her. The heavy impact from his boots echoed against the hospital floor, announcing his presence. "Don't let him take me!" Breeze cried as she looked the doctor in her eyes.

The doctor could see the frightened look on Breeze's face, and she instantly knew that something was not right.

When Ma'tee appeared in the doorway, the doctor looked from Breeze to Ma'tee.

"Is everything okay back here?" he asked.

His voice was eerie and threatening. Breeze's fear of him was so great that she felt like she was having a heart attack. She couldn't stop herself from crying. Zyir was so close. She had heard his voice. *I just needed a few more minutes to tell him where I am,* she thought as she sobbed.

"Everything is fine," the doctor answered nervously. She helped Breeze into the bed and lifted her leg. "She is in a lot of pain, and I haven't administered her any pain medications yet. This type of pain will make a grown man cry. It is not unusual."

"Me need to get her back home. She can recover there," Ma'tee asserted. His tone did not leave room for protest, and he came into the room and sat next to Breeze who trembled timidly from his presence. Ma'tee examined her closely, intimidating her.

The doctor could sense tension in the air. She rubbed Breeze's shoulders. "The anesthesia has she temperature low," the doctor said, covering for Breeze.

Breeze wasn't shaking because she was cold. She was angry. She was terrified. She was praying that Zyir had not hung up his phone and that he could somehow save her.

The doctor looked Breeze directly in the eyes and said, "Everything will be fine. "I'm going to get discharge papers for you to sign, young lady. Me will be right back," she said.

The doctor disappeared, and Ma'tee sat down directly on the bed with her. The smell of him nauseated her and made her skin crawl. He didn't say a word to her, but instead stared at her intensely, trying to determine whether or not she had told anyone anything.

Breeze closed her eyes and thought of Zyir. She recalled his face in her mind, and forced herself to calm down.

The doctor reentered the room. "Oh, please sir. You can wait in the hallway while she dresses. Me will help she, and then get chu de medicine she needs. She will be fine," the doctor said.

Ma'tee reluctantly left the room, but he made sure to watch through the peephole at the top of the door.

The doctor handed Breeze a clipboard. Her hands shook, because something told her that this young girl was in grave danger. She knew who Ma'tee was. Everyone in Haiti knew who he was and what he was capable of. The doctor did not want to get involved out of fear of being hurt herself.

Breeze cried as she took the pen. She wrote her first and last name on the clipboard, and then jotted a quick note.

> *Please help me! Call this number, 1-810-625-1816. Tell him I am alive. I'm trapped somewhere in the mountains. Please!*

Breeze dressed slowly, and then Ma'tee whisked her away from the doctor's office and back up to captivity.

Chapter Seven

The Cartel

"Breeze!" Zyir screamed into the phone as he strained to hear the conversation on the other end of the line. He could barely hear what was going on, but he knew that it was her. He felt it in his gut. She had only said his name, but she was the only person who had the ability to say it so sweetly. "Breeze! Pick up the phone!" he yelled. Tears came to his eyes when the call was disconnected. His heart was beating so rapidly that he had to pull the car over. He hit his steering wheel in frustration. She had called him. He didn't know where she was or why it had taken her so long to reach out to him, but she was alive, and he had to find her. He picked up his phone and speed-dialed Young Carter.

"Zy, how that money looking out in—" Carter started to speak, but Zyir interrupted him.

"She's alive, fam! Breeze is alive, man!" Zyir
stated, getting choked up. After months of her
death haunting him, his faith was restored.
Breeze had been the only chick who had been
able to steal Zyir's focus away from his hustle.
He had nightmares about her death every night.
He felt responsible for what had happened to
her, but now he was sure that she was out there
somewhere, and out of all the people she could
have called, she chose him.

His statement took Carter by surprise. "Zyir,
fam, Breeze is . . ."

"Carter, she called me! She called my fucking
phone! She's alive! I'm on my way to you!" he
screamed urgently.

"I'm not at home. I'm leaving my barber now.
We don't need to meet at the house. Feds are
crawling all over the place. Meet me at Mecca's
money house. I'll give him a call," Carter answered.

Zyir's stomach was hollow as he raced toward
Liberty City where Mecca stashed the drugs and
money that he distributed and collected from the
Lib City hustlers. He beat both Mecca and Carter
there. He scoped the entire block, removed the
money he was transporting, and with the duffel
bag in one hand and his pistol in the other, he
entered the home. He quickly opened the safe

and stuffed the money inside. Carter's rule was to count the cash before putting it away, but Zyir's head was all over the place. He didn't give a fuck about anything or anyone but Breeze.

He paced the living room floor, trying to play back the pieces of conversation he had heard on the phone. "Where is she?" he mumbled to himself. "Think. What did you hear?" he said over and over.

Zyir was driving himself crazy. He was so deep in thought that he didn't even hear Carter come in. Mecca walked in directly behind Carter and they watched as Zyir talked to himself. Carter noticed the worried look on Zyir's face. He had seen Zyir sell crack to his own mother and not bat an eye. He knew his li'l nigga through and through. The look of concern that Zyir held was the same one that Carter felt inside for Miamor. It was then that he knew Zyir's love for Breeze ran deeper than anyone knew.

"Zyir," Carter called out, startling him.

"Fuck is up with you, fam?" Mecca asked.

"Breeze . . . she's still alive," Zyir stated.

A look of anger flickered in Mecca's eyes, and he pointed his finger sternly toward Zyir. "Don't speak her name, nigga. You didn't even know her like that. After eight months, you talking about she's alive!" Mecca said, becoming emotional over his baby sister.

"Fuck you! Bitch-ass nigga!" Zyir yelled back. He didn't give a fuck. He knew Mecca was a killer, but Zyir had been taught to only fear a nigga who didn't bleed. "I just told you your sister is alive! Whether you want to believe it or not, she's out there, and I'm gon' find her!"

Mecca's hands automatically rested on his waist-line for easy access to his burner, but he had to remember that Zyir was family now. That fact alone kept Zyir breathing after disrespecting Mecca, but he was skeptical, and his doubt showed on his face. "She's been gone eight months," Mecca stated sadly.

"She called me!" Zyir yelled.

"She called you?" Mecca answered. "How the fuck you know it ain't one of these lurking-ass mu'fuckas trying to throw you off and set you up? Huh? Why the fuck would she call *you?*"

Carter watched the exchange back and forth as he attempted to figure out where Zyir's logic was coming from. Zyir had never given him a reason to doubt him before, and he was slowly beginning to recall all the time that Zyir and Breeze had spent together.

"It wasn't nobody else. I know her voice, mu'fucka. She called me. She was crying and she said my name. I'm her man, and she needs me! I have to find her, and I'll murk any nigga who tries to stop me!" Zyir said through clenched teeth as he looked Mecca directly in the eyes. Zyir was an emotional wreck. Breeze was still alive, he would put his life on it, and he was willing to go against a thousand armies to get her back. She had been out there alone and vulnerable for eight months, while The Cartel had buried her and moved on.

Seeing Zyir's conviction brought tears to Mecca's eyes, which he quickly brushed away as he felt his anger rise. He wanted to shoot Zyir's ass in the foot for fucking around with his little sister in the first place, but he was glad that she had chose a nigga who was built right, one who was willing to go to the ends of the earth because of a phone call. Breeze had chosen a li'l nigga who Mecca thought their father would have approved of. Mecca nodded his head and looked at Carter, who sat there calmly, grinding his jaw, a clear indication that he was angry.

"We buried her. We counted her out, and she's been out there all this time," Zyir said.

"What did you hear?" Carter asked.

"It was muffled, but it sounded like she was talking to a doctor," Zyir replied.

"Check the hospitals . . . every hospital in the state if you have to," Carter instructed to Zyir. "Mecca, you too, but stay out of Florida. Estes is still on your ass. He's lying low, but that don't mean he's gone. You check hospitals in Georgia and Alabama, and even go as far as Mississippi if nothing shakes. If she's out there, we won't stop until we bring her home. If anyone hears anything, let me be the first to know."

Mecca left in search of his baby sister. It had been a long time since he'd prayed, but for this, he closed his eyes and asked God for help. When he was gone Carter turned to Zyir.

"Why did she call you?" Carter asked. He already knew the answer, but he wanted to see if Zyir would keep it one hundred with him.

Zyir rubbed the top of his head, his eyebrows raised in distress. "I was fucking with her, fam," Zyir admitted.

Carter stood sternly. "And the day she was taken?" Carter asked.

"She was with me," Zyir admitted.

Carter nodded his head.

Zyir could see the fire blazing in his demeanor, but out of respect, he held his tongue.

Carter began to walk out of the house and stopped at the doorway. "Find her," he said simply, then left Zyir to his thoughts.

Zyir searched high and low, visiting hospitals, spending every minute of his day looking for Breeze. He doubted that she was still in the city. He couldn't imagine her being so close for this long without word getting back to The Cartel. He started in the surrounding cities. From Palm Beach to Tampa to Orlando and Ft. Lauderdale, he drove for hours, fighting fatigue on a desperate mission to find her. He had a list of over 100 hospitals in Florida. He called some to see if they had any patients who fit Breeze's description. If there was even a possibility that a patient could be her, then Zyir hit the highway.

After ten hours of disappointments, he had exhausted every hospital on the list, except for the local Miami institutions. He decided to visit Baptist Hospital first.

A tight knot filled his stomach as he whipped his Lexus through the city streets. He was tired, but he couldn't call it a night. He didn't have time to sleep. The thought of Breeze suffering somewhere would not allow him to stop his hunt. He had heard the fear in her voice. Wherever she was, she was in danger and she was defenseless. Every time he closed his eyes, he imagined the terror she may be going through.

Little did he know, he could not fathom what she was being forced to endure. Her fate was worse than death. Her torture was unimaginable.

Zyir pulled into the emergency room parking lot and jumped out. He walked into the hospital. Doubt and apprehension ate away at him as he approached the nurse's station.

"Can I help you, sir?" a young black girl asked without looking up from the paperwork in front of her.

"I'm looking for a girl who may have been treated here. Her name is Breeze Diamond," Zyir stated.

At the mention of the last name "Diamond", the girl looked up. Her eyes scanned Zyir from head to toe. She instantly knew he was a part of The Cartel. Everything about Zyir screamed power, and his swagger made her wet instantly. The young nurse had never had the pleasure of being this close to one of The Cartel's members. She had only heard about their prestige because their reputation rang loudly in every 'hood in Florida. The last name Diamond was associated with money in the city of Miami, but it was an exclusive club, and not everyone had access to them. *Today must be my lucky day,* she thought as she ogled him from head to toe. She put the tip of a pen in her mouth seductively, obviously vying for his attention.

Zyir's patience was non-existent at this point. He was immune to her flirtation. "Look, bitch, I don't got time for all that extra shit. Type in the name and see if she's here," he said crudely without ever raising his voice.

An embarrassed expression appeared on the girl's face as she turned toward the computer. "Breeze Diamond," the girl repeated as she typed the name. She shook her head. "She wasn't treated here. There is no record of a Diamond being admitted."

Zyir massaged his jaw line and hit the desk in frustration, causing the girl to jump. His red eyes were filled with worry. "Look, I need to find her. She's young, light skinned, long curly hair . . . she has a small mole on the side of her neck and a scar on her collarbone. She may not be here under her name. I just need you to check to see if there's anybody here that fits her description. Please!" Zyir said desperately. "It's important!"

The nurse could sense his agony and nodded her head. "Okay. You can have a seat. I'll check."

Zyir sat down with his head in his hands. Minutes passed, but it felt like time was frozen still.

"Sir?" the nurse called to him.

He rushed over to the desk.

"We have a Jane Doe here. She came in a few months ago with no ID, and no one has been here to claim her yet. You can take a look to see if it's who you're looking for," the nurse stated with sympathy.

"Thank you, ma," Zyir stated as he followed her to the elevator and down a long hallway. Zyir breathed deeply. *Please, let this be her!* he said in his mind.

The nurse stopped in front of a room. "I just want to warn you, she's in pretty bad shape. There are injuries to her face and body," the nurse warned.

Zyir wiped his nose and nodded his head to prepare himself for what he was about to see. The nurse opened the door. The room was dark, and the sound of machines beeping was all that could be heard. He stepped closer to the bed, and when the lights turned on, he gasped in shock.

"Is this her?" the nurse asked.

Zyir was at a loss for words as he stared at the woman before him. She was barely recognizable. She looked as if she was hanging onto her life by a thread. He shook his head and backpedaled out of the room. "No, it's not her," he said. He rushed out of the hospital and immediately dialed Carter's number. It was two o'clock in the morning, but it was a phone call that could not wait.

"Hello?" Carter answered groggily.

"Fam, it's me," Zyir said.

"Did you find her?" Carter asked.

"Carter, I found your girl. I found Miamor!"

***

Carter entered the hospital with an entourage of twenty men behind him. Members of The Cartel guarded all entrance and exit points of the building, shutting it down. No one was allowed to enter or exit the premises. Zyir and a select few of Carter's most efficient workers followed him up to the fifth floor where Miamor was located. The same nurse who had assisted Zyir jumped up from her post when she saw the men enter the building. "Excuse me. It's past visiting hours. There are too many of you. You all can't just roam through the hospital," she protested. Carter brushed past her, never even acknowledging her. Zyir put his fingers to his lips and told her, "Sit back down and do your job." He slipped her a stack of money and kept his stride alongside young Carter. "Text Mecca, and tell him to get here quickly," Carter ordered. His Mauri alligator's echoed against the tile floor. His black Armani sweater, white collar shirt and black tie gave him a distinguished look. As he stepped onto the elevator, he was silent, eerily silent, and Zyir knew that once Carter saw Miamor's condition, the entire city of Miami would rain bullets. Zyir hadn't prepared Carter for what he was about to see. He did not want to be the messenger that delivered the bad news. He thought it would be best if Carter saw it for himself. He led Carter to Miamor's room and stopped at the door. The five men who had come up with them dispersed themselves throughout the fifth floor. Zyir posted up outside of the door. "I think you need to go in alone, fam," Zyir said.

Carter entered the room. The smell of death lingered in the air. He walked over to the bed and flipped on the lamp that sat on the stand beside it. When he saw her face, the strong visage he had put on crumbled, and he lowered his head to his chest and squeezed her bed rails in agony. It felt as if someone had knocked the air out of his lungs, and he balled his fist and bit his knuckles to stop his dam of emotions from giving way.

He stared down at his lady . . . the woman he loved. Her face was black and blue, her left eye seemed caved in, and her skin was puffy and swollen with infection. There were parts of her body that were cut deeply, and medical stitches were everywhere. Carter took in every laceration, every cut, every imperfection, and absorbed the pain as his own. He instantly felt guilty, because he could only assume that whoever had done this to her had done so to get to him.

How did I let this happen? He asked himself. He grabbed her hand and noticed how ice cold she was. Her lips were dry and cracked, and her hair was breaking off onto the pillow. *She's been here for three months. I left her here alone, fight-*

ing for her life, Carter thought sadly. He wanted to climb into the bed beside her, but he was afraid that he would hurt her. She looked so fragile, and the many machines and tubes connected to her body prevented him from getting that close.

He pulled a chair near her bedside and sat down. "I'm here, Miamor," he whispered. "I'm right here with you, ma." He brought her hand up and kissed it over and over again as he closed his eyes in defeat. "I'm going to murder the niggas that did this to you. Don't worry about it, ma. I'ma take care of you. I'ma take care of everything!"

Mecca pulled recklessly up to the hospital doors. When he'd gotten the text to come straight to Baptist Hospital, a wave of relief washed over him. He too had been searching all day and night for Breeze. *They found her!* he thought gratefully. He couldn't wait to see her face. He promised himself that now that he had her back, he would never allow anything to happen to her ever again. He left his car at the entrance, causing the security guard to approach him.

"Sir, you need to move your car. You can't park it there."

Mecca noticed some members of The Cartel standing near the entrance, and tossed them his keys. "Take care of it," he instructed as he rushed inside.

When Mecca stepped off of the elevator, he saw Zyir pacing back and forth. He rushed toward him. "Where is she?" Mecca asked.

Zyir nodded his head toward the room door and said, "Carter's inside with her now, but Mecca, it's not—"

Before Zyir could finish his sentence, Mecca rushed inside the room. "Breeze!" he yelled as he rushed over to Carter.

Carter stood suddenly. *He thinks it's Breeze,* he thought as he stood and pushed Mecca backwards. "Mecca, wait . . . it's not her. It's not Breeze."

Mecca pushed past Carter and stopped dead in his tracks when he saw Miamor lying in the bed. Hate filled his heart when he realized who it was, and that his attempts to kill her had failed. "This dirty-ass bitch!" he yelled as he lunged for the bed.

Seeing Mecca's rage toward Miamor sent Carter over the edge. Brother against brother, Carter grabbed Mecca by his neck and slammed him against the wall. Mecca struggled against Carter, but the forearm that was pressed against his throat had him off balance, giving Carter the upper hand.

Carter put his finger in Mecca's face. "Fuck is wrong wit' you, fam?" he seethed, his eyes deadly as he hemmed Mecca up.

Mecca pushed Carter off of him, breathing hard from anger.

"I thought she was Breeze!" Mecca yelled as he punched a hole through the hospital wall. "Fuck!" he screamed as he glared at Miamor and shook his hand in pain. The only thing standing between him bringing her the death that she deserved was his brother, Carter. "You in here worried about this bitch, and my sister is out there somewhere!"

Their confrontation was interrupted when a man entered the room, wearing a lab coat and carrying a chart. "Gentlemen, I'm Doctor Shaw," the white man introduced. "We've been waiting for someone to claim this young woman. You are?"

Mecca glared at Miamor with a hatred that Carter had never seen. Carter contained himself and approached Mecca. He could understand how Miamor had taken Mecca by surprise, but he did not appreciate the disrespect. He took a deep breath, and walked up on him then whispered in his ear. "Now isn't the time or the place for this.

Now, I don't know what the fuck you got against her, but whatever it is, you settle that shit. Now that I found her, she's gon' be around, so get used to it. If you ever come out your mouth again about her, I'ma handle you, my nigga. Believe that. Now, you need to go for a walk. Use all of that energy you got and use it to find Breeze, and put the word out to find the nigga who is responsible for doing this to Miamor." Under normal conditions, Carter would never threaten his brother, but seeing the larceny in Mecca toward Miamor had forced him into a protective rage over his woman.

Mecca stormed out of the room, startling Zyir. "I'ma murder that bitch!" he heard Mecca mumble as he passed by.

Zyir looked back in the room to see what had gone down, but Carter closed the door, then turned to focus his attention on the doctor. He took a deep breath to calm himself before he spoke.

"I apologize for my brother's behavior, Dr. Shaw, I'm Carter Jones," he said as he extended his hand.

"How do you know the patient?" the doctor inquired.

"She's my fiancée," Carter explained. "Can you tell me how this happened? How is she?"

The doctor sighed and checked Miamor's vitals as he began to explain her condition. "No one knows exactly what happened to her, Mr. Jones. She was found like this outside of an abandoned house. She's in a coma. She has severe head trauma, and she's had numerous blood transfusions. She has three broken ribs, and her jawbone is shattered. If she ever wakes up, she may want to consider reconstructive surgery to correct the jaw. She also has chemical poisoning. There were high levels of toxins found in her blood. Whoever did this to her never intended for her to survive. She's strong. I have never seen someone hold on for this long after everything she's been through."

Carter found the news extremely hard to hear, and his stomach was in knots as he stared at Miamor. "Will she ever wake up?"

The doctor sighed. "That I cannot answer for you. The good news is we ran a CT scan on her, which revealed high levels of brain activity. She's thinking, and still has the capacity to function mentally. She may even be able to hear you, but for some reason right now she can't come into a conscious state. Only time will tell."

Carter found the news extremely hard to bear. He put his hand on his head, rubbing the waves on his freshly cut Caesar, and took a deep breath. "The machines?" he asked, his voice cracking from emotion. He cleared his throat and continued, "Why is she hooked up to so many machines?"

"One of her lungs isn't functioning properly. We have her on a ventilator to ensure that she is getting enough oxygen. Once the lung heals and kicks back in, she should be able to breathe on her own. Until then, I will do all that I can to make her comfortable," the doctor said with sympathy.

Carter shook his head. "Thank you, Dr. Shaw, but I'm taking her home where I know she will be safe." Carter walked out of the room to where Zyir was waiting in the hallway with a briefcase in his hands. Carter took the case and popped it open. Inside, $100,000 lay in neat bundles. "I'm sure this will take care of any resources that your hospital has used to treat her."

Despite the doctor's protests, Carter took Miamor back to the Diamond Estate. He had a room set up for her where all of her medical needs would be met. He sat down next to Miamor's bed. The night had been long, and the sunrise crept over the horizon and illuminated the room as he gripped her hand, his emotions running wild. A 9 mm sat in his lap. The hum of the medical machines was torture to his ears.

First Breeze, now this, Carter thought, overwhelmed. He hadn't found peace since he had come to Miami. He did not know how his father had ever handled the massive empire that he had built with such ease. Carter felt like everything and everyone he loved was slipping through his fingers. *Maybe this is why my father walked away from my mother, so that he would not have to watch her suffer at the hands of the game. I should have followed my first mind and kept Miamor at a distance. If I had walked away from her, this would have never happened,* he thought miserably. His father's logic made much more sense to him now as he watched Miamor fight for her life.

He lowered his head and rested his face in the palm of his hands. He picked up his cell and dialed Mecca's number. He needed his brother. He couldn't handle all of the chaos alone, and he was not trying to lose the only family he had left.

Carter did not know that in order to keep Miamor, he was going to have to let Mecca go. He would eventually have to choose one or the other, because there was no way that Mecca and Miamor could ever co-exist.

Mecca sent Carter to voice mail as he pushed his Lamborghini through the streets. His foot was like lead on the gas pedal. There was only

one thing on his mind . . . murder. He called
Fabian repeatedly, but never got an answer.

*Bitch-ass nigga couldn't handle one fucking
job. Kill the bitch! That's all I asked him to do,*
he thought.

His luxury whip left rubber on the ground
beneath him as he made his way to his destination. He pulled up to an apartment community
and slammed his car door furiously as he made
his way inside. Too impatient to wait for the
elevator, he stormed up the stairway all the way
to the seventh floor. He found apartment 7B.

Knock! Knock!

Fabian opened the door, keeping the security
chain in place, but when he saw Mecca's face, he
tried to close it quickly.

Mecca pushed his way into the apartment,
causing the door to hit Fabian in the face.

"Oww, shit!" Fabian grimaced as he held his
nose and backed up into the apartment. M-M-
M-Mecca! What's good, homeboy? Fuck is all
this for?" Fabian stuttered nervously while blood
leaked from his busted nose.

Mecca didn't say a word. He removed his .38
and then began to screw the silencer on as his
eyes burned a hole through Fabian, daring him
to move.

"Mecca, man! Please, man!" Fabian begged.

Mecca aimed his pistol at Fabian's head and fired two shots. The only sound that could be heard was Fabian's body hitting the floor, and just as quickly as Mecca had come, he left. He had no regrets and no remorse. All he wanted was revenge. He knew that talking to Carter was useless. Miamor had him blinded. Carter had placed Miamor on a pedestal so high that he refused to see the truth, but Mecca was determined to get to her. *As soon as the nigga turns his back, I'ma murder his bitch.*

Dr. Nataya Azor walked into her practice and sighed. She knew that today would be a long and dreadful day. She hadn't gotten much sleep last night, thinking about the young girl she had treated the day before. She knew for a fact that Ma'tee was not the girl's father, but she wanted to stay out of it. She wanted no part of whatever was going on. To get into the business of a man as ruthless as Ma'tee could put her in a bad position. She could easily come up missing if she chose to intervene. She tried her best to ignore the situation, but then she thought of her own beautiful children. *If they were in trouble, I would not want another mother to turn a blind eye to dem,* she thought with indecision. Dr. Azor had gotten the message that Breeze had written her, but fear had stopped her from making the call on the girl's behalf. She had tried to put the note in the back of her mind and remain professional, but all night she tossed and turned, thinking of the look of terror she had witnessed in Breeze's eyes. She looked at the clock. She still had an hour before her office opened. She put her things down and walked over to the file cabinet where she kept her patients' files. She flipped through them until she retrieved what she was looking for. "Breeze Diamond," she whispered aloud. Her mind told her to put the file away and go about her day, but the motherly instinct in her forced her to find Breeze's note. She took a deep breath and picked up the phone, but quickly changed her mind and slammed it back down. Her foot tapped nervously against the floor as she contemplated on what to do. She read the note again: *Please help me! Call this number. 1-810-625-1816. Tell him I am alive. I'm trapped somewhere in the mountains. Please!*

"One phone call will not hurt," she said. She picked up the phone and slowly dialed the number, silently hoping that no one would answer.

"Hello?"

"Please listen carefully. A girl by the name of Breeze was treated in me doctor's office yesterday. She asked me to call this number. She's in danger. She's is in Haiti. Ma'tee has her trapped in de mountains," Dr. Azor said.

"Who is this?" Zyir shouted as he sat straight up in his bed, but all he got in response was a dial tone. He immediately threw on some jeans and his kicks and grabbed his keys. *Haiti!* he thought in despair. *What the fuck? Ma'tee?* Zyir knew that if what the caller said was true, then Breeze was in much more danger than anyone could have ever imagined, and he had to get to her . . . before it was too late.

Chapter Eight

The Cartel

Breeze began to feel better, and Ma'tee had allowed her to roam free in the secluded basement without being bound to the bed. It had been a week since she was at the hospital, and she couldn't stop thinking about Zyir's voice. She knew that she had blown the only chance that she had to be saved. She paced the room back and forth as she tried to think of a way out of the clutches of Ma'tee, but she was beginning to realize that she would never escape. He was in complete control, and had become obsessed with her. She broke down into tears as she began to accept her reality. "I would rather die!" she whispered as she felt like giving up on life. She was a Diamond, and she took pride in that name. She would rather die on her feet rather than live on her knees. She, at that moment, gave up on life.

The sound of the door unlocking startled her, and she stared at the steps until she saw the feet of Ma'tee emerging. He walked down, smiling as if he was a husband coming home to his wife.

"I hate you!" Breeze whispered as she backed into a corner, watching him walking toward her. She saw the look in his eyes, and already knew what his intentions were. He came down there for sex. "No, Ma'tee! Don't do this!" she begged as she held her hands out in front of her.

"Relax, beautiful gal," Ma'tee said as he licked his lips and thought about how good it felt to be inside of Breeze's tight wound. He had broken her virginity months ago, but every time seemed like the first time to him.

Breeze learned that fighting back only made it worse for her, so she reluctantly got up and walked toward the bed. Ma'tee followed closely behind her and began to rub her behind. He relieved her of her gown and looked at her naked, slender body as she lay on the bed. Tears were running down her face, but he paid them no mind as he prepared to have his way with her. He dropped his pants and began to degrade her.

Ma'tee went down on her and performed oral sex on her as she laid there not responding to him at all. Her legs shook, not in pleasure but in fear as he ate her out sloppily. Tears ran down her face as she had no choice but to submit to Ma'tee.

Zyir's heart raced as he waited patiently for Mecca to return. He had been blowing his phone up, trying to let him know that Breeze was alive and somewhere in Haiti. Zyir looked at Carter, who was coming down the stairs while talking on a cell phone. Carter was scheduling a helicopter to drop them off in Haiti. Zyir had never come clean about everything that happened on the night that Breeze was kidnapped. Carter and Mecca knew that he was the last one with Breeze that night, but what Zyir didn't tell them was that he was in the process of taking Breeze's virginity. Their sexual act had caused his distraction, and his sloppiness had led to her being taken. *How would he take it?* Zyir asked himself as he buried his face in his hands. He quickly shook off the feeling of overwhelming guilt and focused on the positive; Breeze was alive.

"Did you get in touch with Mecca?" Carter asked as he flipped down his phone and grabbed a phone book.

"I can't reach him. I've been trying to call him all morning, but he's not answering the phone," Zyir said as he stood up and began to pace the floor. He picked up the phone and tried to reach Mecca once again, but he just got the voice-mail like before. "Damn! We are just going to have to go without him," Zyir said as he pulled his gun out, ready to kill whatever and whoever to get Breeze back.

Carter ran his finger down the phonebook's page, searching for a home health aide. He didn't want to leave Miamor there alone without help. He wanted her to see a friendly face if she awoke from her coma, rather than one of his goons that he had guarding her room.

He glanced over at Zyir, who was pacing the floor, looking nervous and anxious. Carter stopped what he was doing and walked over to him. He put his hand on Zyir's shoulder and stopped him in his tracks. "You got to calm down. I want you to relax and take a step back. We don't know what we are about to walk into when we get to Haiti, so we have to be ready for whatever. But we will most definitely be at a disadvantage if you're all riled up. Fall back, fam," Carter said as he watched Zyir letting his emotions get the best of him. "You really cared for her, huh?" Carter asked as he looked at Zyir and saw the flame in his eyes.

"Yeah, we were getting close, ya know. This shit ain't for her, man. I'm ready to go get her," Zyir said seriously, looking his mentor in the eyes.

Before Carter could respond, the door opened and in came Mecca.

"Yo, Mecca! We got her. We know where she's at," Carter said.

Mecca smiled as his trigger finger began to itch. He would deal with Miamor when he got back. Now it was time for him to get his sister back. "Let's go get my baby sister," he said in a low raspy tone as he pulled out his gun and cocked it back. He felt his heart flutter at the sound of Carter's words. She was the only remaining full-blooded sibling he had left, and he was determined to bring her back home where she belonged.

Carter, Zyir, and Mecca rode in the aircraft that flew 1,500 feet above land, all of them wearing headphones to drown out the overwhelming loud noise of the helicopter's propeller. Carter had rented a private helicopter to make this trip to Haiti in the hope of finding Breeze. Everyone remained silent as they watched the pilot maneuver the aircraft over the ocean. The light blue water beneath seemed so beautiful, but none of them had beautiful thoughts on their minds; only murderous ones. The helicopter finally cleared the water, and the beautiful island of Haiti was now visible. The tall exotic trees and dirt trails took up most of the land, and the pilot spotted a safe landing spot in the middle of the town of Saint-Marcs, a city in the middle of the island. It was also the same place that Breeze was treated. With their connections, they found the exact location where the call was from. They all were anxious as the helicopter swayed back and forth as it prepared to land. As the helicopter hovered over the open field, the grass blew wildly because of the velocity of the chopper's propellers. Carter cocked his gun back, making sure he was locked and loaded. He didn't know if they were walking into a trap, so he was getting himself prepared for whatever. Zyir and Mecca followed suit and did the same thing. Once the helicopter landed, they all hopped out, and Carter instructed the pilot to wait there for them to return, and left him with a rubberband roll full of money; ten thousand dollars to be exact. Zyir grabbed the duffle bag that was full of extra ammunition and automatic guns, preparing for whatever Ma'tee would have in store for them.

The hot, muggy climate and Haiti's air felt different from Miami's air as the sweat began to drip from their brows. They made their way toward the dirt roads that led to the buildings that were just a mile down.

Carter spotted a tall building that resembled a small, rundown hospital, and pointed. "Is that the place right there?" He asked Zyir, and he used his other hand to block the sun from his eyes.

"I think so. The nurse said there is only one doctor's office in the entire town," Zyir said as he looked toward the building and pulling out a small piece of paper.

Just as they were making their way to the building, a young boy ran across the road while kicking a soccer ball.

"Ayo, li'l man!" Carter yelled, trying to get the young boy's attention.

The boy didn't seem any older than ten years old. He was very skinny and had nappy, small beads on his head that was his hair. He stopped kicking the ball and looked at Carter. "Me?' he asked as he looked around and pointed at himself.

"Yeah, you," Carter said as he unleashed a smile. The boy, without fear, picked up his ball and walked toward them.

"What up, mon?" the boy said in his heavy Haitian accent.

"You want to make some money, baby boy?" Carter asked as he reached into his pocket.

The young boy's eyes followed Carter's hands. Carter pulled out a roll of money, and the young boy's eyes grew as large as golf balls. He had never seen a man carry so much money in his entire life. Wealth was not something common in Haiti, and the boy was astonished. "Wow!" he said as he snatched the money from Carter. "Yeah, mon, I want to make dis money!" His eyes were glued on the big-faced bills that were in his hands.

"Okay, well I need your help," Carter said as he placed his hand on the boy's shoulder.

"Anyt'ing, mon! Chu' just name it!" he said energetically.

"I need you to take me to . . ." Carter started to say just before he looked at Zyir for the name of the hospital.

"Hondas Hospital," Zyir said, reading the piece of paper that he had pulled from his pocket.

"Hondas is down the road," he said as he pointed north, in the opposite direction where they thought the hospital was.

"Show us," Carter said as they followed the boy's finger." What's your name, li'l man?" Carter asked.

"Ziggy," he said with his rabbit-like two front teeth.

"All right, Ziggy. We following you," Carter said as he urged Mecca and Zyir to follow him.

Mecca frowned up his face and pulled Carter close as he began to whisper. "How we know this li'l nigga ain't taking us into a trap?" he asked as he kept his eyes open.

"You don't trust anybody, do you?" Carter asked smiling. "Let's just follow him. How else are we going to find our way around?" Carter said, giving Mecca reason to see things his way.

"All right, Carter. But if this li'l nigga on any bullshit, I won't hesitate to blow his shit back," Mecca said as he patted the gun that was on his waist.

Carter shook his head and continued to follow the young boy up the path. *That nigga doesn't have a conscience*, Carter thought. *I'm glad he is on my team, rather than against me.*

After about fifteen minutes of walking, they reached the small hospital. It was a rundown building that resembled a plantation style house more than an actual hospital.

"Here it goes," Ziggy said, pointing at the front door.

"Let's go," Carter said as he hurried into the building, looking for the nurse that called them. He told Ziggy to wait for them on the outside, and whistle if anybody comes in. He slipped him another hundred dollar bill for good measure.

Ziggy proudly accepted the responsibility as the watchman, and smiled proudly as he stuck out his chest and answered, "Yes sir!"

Carter, Zyir, and Mecca rushed through the hospital, all of them with gun in hand.

Mecca called the doctor's name loudly, and his voice echoed throughout the halls. "Where is the nurse that called us?" he yelled as loud and clear as he could.

Nurses and patients gasped at the sight of the men mobbing through the place like they owned it. A woman emerged from one of the rooms, and Mecca immediately knew that she was the person that they were looking for.

"May I help you?" she asked, frowning in confusion.

"Are you the nurse that called?" Mecca asked as he gripped his pistol and pointed it directly at her. Carter quickly placed his hand on Mecca's gun and lowered it for him.

"Yes, I'm Azor," she answered with fear all over her face and shaking limbs.

"Relax!" Carter said under his breath, as he knew Mecca was at his boiling point, ready to shoot whomever. "Let me handle this," he said, just before he focused his attention on the doctor. "Azor?" Carter asked the lady as he stared at her with kind eyes.

"Yes, that's me. Let's talk in here," Azor said, and she opened up an empty room. They all followed her in, and the doctor closed the door after she looked around to make sure that the coast was clear.

"You called my man right here, and said that a young lady was in this place, right?" Carter asked as he placed his hand on her shoulder to calm her. She was noticeably shaken up.

"Yes, I did," she said.

"Is this the young lady you saw?" Carter asked, wanting to make sure that it was Breeze. He pulled a picture out of his pocket of Breeze. It was one of her senior picture she had taken years before. The doctor stared at the picture for a minute and nodded her head to verify that it was her.

"Where is she?" Mecca interrupted, as he quickly grabbed the nurse by her hair and put the gun to her temple. The nurse instantly put her hands up and began to cry out of pure fear.

"What the fuck you doing?" Zyir asked in confusion as he saw the murderous look in Mecca's eyes.

"Fall back, Mecca!" Carter yelled as he put his hand up to signal Mecca to stop.

"No, fuck that! My sister is alive, and this bitch is going to take me to her!" Mecca screamed as the veins in his neck and forehead began to slightly bulge out.

The doctor's words got caught in her throat as she tried to give Mecca the best answer she knew. "She is with Ma'tee. That' all I know. Ma'tee is a very powerful man in this town, and all that I know is that he lives somewhere in the Black Mountains. You have to go up the mountain and through the jungle to get to his place," she said quickly.

"Where's that at?" Carter asked as he listened closely while Mecca still had a tight grip on her.

"It's five miles down the road and up the mountain. It's barricaded, so no cars can get through. You will have to hike the trail and climb the mountain to get there," she said as tears streamed down her face. Her hands shook nervously, and she flinched at every little movement that Mecca made.

Carter heard enough, and headed out. "Come on, Mecca," he said as he opened the door.

"If you are lying, I will come back and kill you and your whole family," Mecca said, meaning every word that came out of his mouth. He unleashed the doctor and headed outside.

Carter rushed outside and went directly to Ziggy, who was waiting for him on the steps of the hospital. "Ziggy, I need you, li'l man," Carter said.

"Anything. What chu want?" he asked.

"Do you know how to get to the Black Mountains?" he asked.

"You mean Ma'tee's place?" Ziggy asked as he scratched his head.

His statement was music to their ears. They knew that they were about find Breeze and bring her home at that point.

Zyir was beaming on the inside. He knew that it was a chance for him to reunite with the woman he loved; Breeze. "Yeah, you know where it's at?" Zyir asked.

"I know exactly how to get there," Ziggy said as he headed north toward the Black Mountains.

Chapter Nine

The Cartel

Breeze cried as she watched Ma'tee pull up his pants and look down at her. There was no remorse on his face. The fact that he was killing her slowly on the inside meant nothing to him. The sweat from his brow dripped down his dark face, causing Breeze's stomach to turn in disgust. The sick smile that he wore terrified her. He was so sure of himself . . . so proud of the sexual acts he had forced upon her. Ma'tee had even gone as far as to ejaculate inside of young Breeze, in a twisted attempt to impregnate her. He knew that a child would join them together forever, and that was his ultimate goal. Without saying a word, he walked away and up the stairs. Breeze heard the sounds of Ma'tee locking the deadbolts that trapped her in the basement.

Breeze sat up and began to cry. She felt so violated and dirty. Ma'tee had degraded her on many occasions, and she was forced to give her virginity to a man that she hated; the same man that was responsible for her father's death. She got on her knees and began to pray to God, hoping that her father also heard her prayers. She was at a point where she didn't want to live anymore. Her regard for life was slowly fading.

The longer she stared at the four walls of her imprisonment, the more her mind abandoned her. Breeze knew that if she didn't find a way out, then she would go insane.

She finished her prayer and got up to walk to the bathroom that was connected to the basement. She stood over the sink and looked at her reflection in the mirror. Her eyes were bloodshot and swollen from her endless crying, and as she stared at the woman in the mirror, she couldn't even recognize herself. She was not the same girl. The young woman staring back at her was not Breeze Diamond. At that point, she realized that she had not looked at herself in almost a year. Every time she used the bathroom, she would just avoid eye contact with the mirror, almost as if she were ashamed. Ma'tee had stripped her of her innocence a long time ago, and she was not who she once was. The naïveté of a young little rich girl had disappeared. She now knew pain. She now knew what war really was. She now knew loneliness.

"Diamonds are forever!" she whispered as she wiped away her tears and repeated a motto that her father would always say to her as a young girl. She knew that she had the blood of a king, and at that moment, refused to let Ma'tee hurt her anymore.

She glanced over at the corner of the room and saw something that could possibly help her escape Ma'tee grasp. She took a deep breath and walked toward it. She had just gotten an idea.

Sweat dripped off of each of the men as they tried to keep up with little Ziggy as he walked up the rocky trail. The trail wrapped around the tall mountain, and the sun was just setting. "Come on, guys. We have to beat the sun," Ziggy emphasized as he led the way, while holding a big stick in his hand.

Carter took off his shirt as the sweat cascaded down his body. They had been climbing the mountain for nearly two hours, and the air was getting thinner as they got higher up in altitude.

"You sure this is the way, li'l man," Zyir asked as his legs grew tired.

"Yeah, I'm sure. Me and me friends used to come and play in this jungle every day. We snooped around here last summer when Ma'tee

was away in Miami. We're almost there," Ziggy
said, showing no sign of being winded.

On the other hand, the rest of them were
exhausted, but their love for Breeze kept them
going. Zyir couldn't wait to hold Breeze in his
arms and tell her that he loved her. He was going
to be her knight in shining armor and save her.
That thought alone made him put some pep
in his step as he sped up, trying to reach their
destination.

Mecca's mind was on shooting Ma'tee right
in between the eyes. Breeze was his only full-
blooded sibling that was still alive, and he would
die if that was the cost of getting her back. *"Here
I come, Breeze,* he thought as he climbed the
trail.

Carter swatted the unfamiliar flying insects
away from his face as he looked up and saw the
abundance of tropical trees.

"Here is de' jungle," Ziggy said as he stopped
and pointed to the woods. "Ma'tee's house is
straight ahead. Just stay north."

Carter stopped and caught his breath, along
with Zyir and Mecca. He then looked at Ziggy
and rubbed the top of his head. "Thanks, Ziggy.
You are real li'l nigga," he said as he smiled. Carter reached around his wrist and pulled off his
designer watch and handed it to Ziggy. "That's

yours," he said as he watched Ziggy admire it like it was a masterpiece. "Now, you have to take off," he told him, and stepped to the side so that Ziggy could go back down the mountain.

"Thanks Ca'ter!" Ziggy said, mispronouncing his name because of his accent. Then Ziggy smiled and ran up and hugged him. "But remember, you have to follow de dirt path or chu will get lost. De jungle is a big circle, mon," he reminded him as he headed back down.

Carter watched as Ziggy disappeared down the trail, then focused back on Mecca and Zyir. "Let's go get Breeze," he said, and they ran through the jungle, following the trail.

After fifteen minutes of running full speed down the trail through the jungle, they saw the house. They all stopped in their tracks when they saw the gigantic house that was before them. They had expected Ma'tee's house to be guarded and surrounded by gates, but to their surprise, it was wide open and unguarded.

Zyir dropped the bag on the ground that he was carrying, which was full of the automatic guns and bullets. He opened the bag, giving a variety of choices to Carter and Mecca. Mecca opted for the 12 gauge, and Carter got the AK 47 assault rifle, also known as a "chopper" because of its ability to spit bullet after bullet, chopping up whatever is in its path. They all strapped up and headed to the house. They were about to go in with guns blazing.

Breeze smiled as she thought about escaping Ma'tee's wrath. It would soon be over, and she would be a free woman. She looked down from the chair she was standing on and wrapped the belt around her neck. Ma'tee had left this leather belt down there after he had sex with her. Little did he know that he had provided Breeze an exit by doing so. Breeze tugged on the belt to make sure that it was wrapped around the pipes above her head securely. Tears began to fall down her face as she shook nervously. The only thing she would have to do was kick the chair out from under her feet, and the nightmare would finally end.

Carter put three fingers up, signaling the countdown. Mecca stood at the front door with a 12 gauge shotgun, aiming it at the lock. Zyir held two pistols in his hands, ready to rush in right after Mecca blew the door open. "Three, two, one!" Carter whispered.

Boom!

Mecca blew through the lock and they all rushed in.

Ma'tee heard the blast while he was in the shower washing the smell of sex off of his body. He quickly turned off the shower and ran into his room that was attached to the bathroom. He reached for the tech-nine automatic handgun he kept under his pillow. He looked at the monitors that were on his wall and gasped. He had his entire house under surveillance, and saw three men running through the downstairs of his home with guns.

"What de blood clot!' he yelled as he held his gun in his hand while dripping wet, and still completely naked. He looked at the security monitor that was watching the basement where he kept Breeze. Ma'tee's heart skipped a beat and he gasped at what he was witnessing. He gripped the sides of the monitor in anguish at the sight of Breeze's feet swinging from the ceiling. He was witnessing her committing suicide. "Nooo!" he yelled as he rushed downstairs to save her. He didn't care that he was going up against three guns, he just wanted to save his love before she died. "Breeze!" he yelled as he ran down the stairs, gun in hand.

Mecca was the first to spot Ma'tee, and reacted without thought or hesitation. He cocked the shotgun back and let off a round, just barely missing Ma'tee. Ma'tee returned fire, spraying anything he saw moving as he made his way down the stairs. Zyir also opened fire as he came from the opposite corner of the room. He hit Ma'tee in the arm, sending him flying down the stairs violently. Carter was toward the back of the house, and came running when he heard the gunshots.

Ma'tee dropped his gun as tumbled down the stairs, leaving a bloody trail behind him. He landed at the bottom of the stairs awkwardly. "Hmm!" he grunted as he tried to sit up and gather his bearings. When he looked up, Mecca was standing over him with a shotgun to his face.

"Where is Breeze?" Mecca screamed as he dug the barrel into on one of Ma'tee's eyes. Before Ma'tee could say anything Mecca kicked him forcefully in his temple out of anger. His emotions got the best of him, and he could not contain himself. Ma'tee was the man who had caused his family grief like no other, and his rage emerged like a bolt of lightning, striking hard and swift. "Where is she?" he yelled as he looked at Ma'tee, who seemed to be losing consciousness.

Ma'tee was dizzy because of the blows Mecca had just given him. He could barely speak. "Breeze!"

he whispered as he thought about her hanging in the basement.

"Fuck that! Breeze!" he yelled as he ran up the stairs, skipping two at a time in a desperate race to find his girl. Carter headed to the back of the gigantic house screaming her name also.

"Breeze!" Zyir yelled as he invaded every room of the house. His heart pounded furiously in his chest, and his instincts told him that something was wrong. *If she's here, why isn't she answering?* He thought. "She's not up here! I can't find her!" he screamed as he descended the steps in worry.

Mecca saw the look in Zyir's eyes, and knew that something was wrong. "Where is she?" Mecca shouted as he looked down at Ma'tee, gripping him by his dreadlocks.

"In . . . the . . . basement," Ma'tee mumbled as blood dripped from his head.

"She's in the basement!" Mecca yelled just before he sent a shotgun blast through Ma'tee's chest, killing him on contact.

Carter rushed to the front, and Mecca told him that she was in the basement. They all rushed to the back of the house and tried to open the basement door, but it was secured with five dead bolts.

"Stand back!" Carter said as he pointed his gun at the lock. He let of five rounds, breaking each lock with each bullet he fired.

"I love you, Poppa. I love you, Mama. I love you, Mecca. I love you, Monroe. I love you, Uncle Polo. I love you, Carter," Breeze whispered, giving each one of her loved ones a personal and final good-bye. She put her hand over her heart and wished that Zyir would've come and saved her. She wished that when she called, she could have gotten the chance to let him know exactly where she was, but she didn't, and now she was about to make her grand exit from her hell on earth. "I love you, Zyir," she added just before she prepared to take her own life. She heard gunshots coming from upstairs, but she was so focused on what she was about to do that she paid them no mind. Breeze kicked the chair from underneath her and her body immediately dropped and dangled from the pipes. She began to squirm and hold her neck. The kiss of death gripped at her body. The pain was so great that she almost regretted her decision, but she would rather face a few moments of it then a lifetime of grief in the shackles of Ma'tee. The pressure building in her head was so great that she began to see stars. Each second was agonizingly slow as her lungs begged her to inhale. The strength of human will caused her to grab at the belt to avoid the suffocation. Her nails broke from grabbing at the leather, and she kicked wildly as the pulse in her head became audible in her own ears. She could hear her heartbeat fading, and just as she was on the brink of unconsciousness, she heard Zyir calling her name. "Breeze! I'm coming!" Zyir's voice came from upstairs.

Zyir! That's Zyir! she thought as she continued to struggle for air. She heard someone trying to get to the basement, but the locks were stopping them.

"Breeze!" Zyir yelled again as he tried to kick the door down. She jerked and contorted her body, trying to release herself, but it didn't work. Frantic and out of air, she grabbed at the belt around her neck, scratching her skin as she attempted to create some slack in the belt. Her world became gray, and her eyes felt like they would pop out of her skull as she put the last bit of strength she had into freeing herself. Her efforts were in vain. It was too late. She was already in the Grim Reaper's hands, and there was nothing she could do. She tried to yell for Zyir, but her airway was cut off. She only could let out small grunts. Her grunts were too low for anyone to hear, and she felt herself slipping away. She couldn't take it anymore, and she finally stopped struggling as life left her body.

Zyir pushed the door open and was the first to head down the stairs. He held his gun in front of him as he crept down the stairs, not knowing who was down there. Carter and Mecca followed closely behind him. Zyir got to the bottom step and his heart broke in two at the sight before him. Breeze was swinging from a ceiling pipe, swinging slowly from left to right. He quickly dropped his gun and ran over to her lifeless body.

"Breeze! Nooo!" he yelled as he held her up by her legs trying to stop her from choking, but it was far too late; she was already gone.

Carter saw Zyir holding Breeze and quickly ran over and picked up the chair so he could stand on it and untie her. His hands shook as he looked at Breeze's limp body.

Mecca was still by the stairs, frozen in heartache. He dropped to his knees and silently cried as he watched his sister's body drop into Zyir's arms. Zyir had never mourned anything or anyone in his life, but as he sat with Breeze in his arms, he rubbed her face as tears flowed down his cheeks. He kissed the top of her head over and over again as he rocked her back and forth while whispering her name again and again. "It wasn't supposed to go down like this!" he whispered into her ear. "Not like this!" he repeated as he wept over her. He looked down at the only girl who had ever stolen his heart and regretted the day he had ever met her. He had never felt a pain so great before she had entered his life. "I'm so sorry, Breeze. This is all my fault," he whispered as he closed his eyes tightly and tried to get the image of her suicide out of his brain.

"Zy," Carter began. He inched closer to Zyir. "Let her go, fam. This ain't on you. Just hand her to me," Carter instructed, seeing that his protégé's grief was as great as his own.

"Don't take her from me, man, not yet. Just don't touch her!" Zyir spoke in a low tone. "She needed me. She was hopeless and she killed herself because I wasn't there." Zyir sat with Breeze for an hour before Carter could convince him that it was time for them to depart. Zyir even tried to give Breeze CPR. They all knew that it was useless, but Zyir wouldn't stop until he tried everything to bring her back. She held the key to his heart, and now that she was gone, it would be locked forever. The beautiful Breeze Diamond was dead.

Chapter Ten

The Cartel

All with tears in their eyes, Mecca, Carter and Zyir walked down the dirt path that led to their awaiting helicopter. They had just climbed down the mountain, none of them saying anything to each other on their way down. Breeze's limp, lifeless body was in Zyir's arms as he carried her with strength, determined to hold her upright and comfortable, even though it was in vain.

The town's patrons followed as they saw Zyir carrying the dead body. It looked as if a parade was going on, with Carter, Zyir, and Mecca leading the pack.

Mecca held his gun out in the open as he walked in broad daylight, with onlookers looking at them in disbelief. With tears flowing, he promised himself that anyone he saw that resembled a Haitian would die in honor of his hatred for Ma'tee. Mecca was at a point where he didn't give a fuck about human life anymore. He was already ruthless, but he had crossed the line, graduating to psychotic. He just wanted somebody to pay for all the grief that Ma'tee and his Haitian mob had caused his family. It seemed as if every Haitian resembled Ma'tee, and Mecca wanted vengeance.

He saw a spectator with a head full of dreads on the side of the road, along with the crowd. Mecca was going all out in tribute to Breeze.

He glanced at her body, and the sight of the red belt marks around her neck made him sick to his stomach. That sight was the most hurtful thing he had ever seen. He knew that Breeze loved herself too much to kill herself. For her to commit suicide, life had to be unbearable. This thought infuriated Mecca and pushed him to his boiling point. He looked back at the dread head and let him have it. Mecca pointed and fired, catching him in the chest. Although the man had no association with Ma'tee and posed no harm, Mecca didn't care. He was borderline insane at that point. As the thunderous sound of the gunshot echoed through the air, people began to scream in horror and run for cover as Mecca looked for any other Haitian that even resembled Ma'tee.

The gunshots didn't bother Carter or Zyir. Usually they would try to tame Mecca, but this time they let his rage flow uninhibited. Neither of them even flinched as Mecca let off round after round, while never stopping his slow pace as they walked. They knew that Mecca was creating therapy for himself in some sort of sick way. Who were they to tell him how to grieve? They were both heartbroken, and the only thing on their minds was getting Breeze back to the States for a proper burial.

Zyir cried silently and kissed Breeze on the forehead while she was in his arms. "I love you," he repeatedly whispered to her as he continued down the trail.

Mecca continued to shoot calmly, with no expression on his face. People were yelling in terror and scattered like roaches as Mecca continued his therapy session.

They reached the helicopter, and the driver was waiting, just as Carter had told him to.

"I can't do this anymore," Carter whispered to himself, referring to burying loved ones. It was as if a healed wound was reopened when they saw Breeze's body hanging from that belt. They had to suffer her death twice, and it was taking a toll on what was left of The Cartel.

They entered the helicopter and the pilot carried them back to the States. The chopper ride remained silent and painful, as tears fell down all of their cheeks.

Carter, Mecca and Zyir stood over the hole in the graveyard. Two of the graveyard's workers began to dump dirt on the cherry oak casket that contained Breeze's body. Breeze's headstone was next to the rest of the Diamond family. Mecca looked at all the tombstones, and noticed that he was the last one left alive with the Diamond bloodline, besides Carter. Zyir stared, as the dirt getting dumped on top of the casket and the flowers that he laid on top of it, slowly disappeared with each scoop. Nothing was said. Each of them were entertaining their own thoughts and grieving within themselves. They all had stonecold stares with heavy hearts. They were all cried out, and at that moment, they knew that The Cartel was over. All of the heartache and anguish wasn't worth it. "I'm done," Mecca said as he stared at the hole in the ground. "Me too . . . me too," Carter whispered as he threw his arm around his brother. "This game is so cold. It wasn't supposed to be like this. We supposed to pop champagne and live the life; but not this. The game has no loyalty," Zyir added as he fought back a single tear for Breeze. Carter began to think about Miamor, and how he had left her there alone for the past couple of days when they had gone to Haiti, and then took care of Breeze's burial. He was fed up and ready to move on and start a life with Miamor.

He looked over at Zyir, the only real nigga he had besides Mecca. He didn't want Zyir to fall victim to the game, and promised himself at that moment that he would not let Zyir fall into the pitfalls of this game.

They stayed there for hours and mourned her death before they headed back to the Diamond residence. Carter knew he would have to start making plans for his exit out of the drug game.

Carter pulled into the Diamond Estate, and the gates were opened by one of his many henchmen that he had guarding the house. Carter gave him a nod and pulled up the long, curvy driveway. He had just dropped Zyir off at his condo, and Mecca decided to stay over at Zyir's. Mecca was acting strange in Carter's eyes. Carter chalked Mecca's awkwardness up to him mourning his sister's suicide. But little did Carter know, Mecca wanted to stay away from Miamor, because he knew that he would eventually kill her if he stayed under the same roof as her. Mecca wanted to wait until she woke from her coma before he killed her. He wanted Miamor to see his eyes as he sent her to her Maker. He was determined to finish the job Fabian had failed to do. Carter got out of his car and entered the house. When he walked in, his henchmen were all on the couch, playing a video game. They were so busy ranting and raving that they didn't notice him come in. "What the fuck is going on here?" he asked loudly, startling all five of the henchmen. They quickly jumped up, sensing the hostility in Carter's voice. "We were just—" the henchmen said, just before Carter threw up his hand, dismissing whatever he had to say. He began to walk over to the crowd of men with both hands behind his back. His body gestures didn't display anger, but the veins that were forming in his neck and forehead was a sure giveaway. "Who is watching Miamor?" he asked calmly, as he looked each one of them in their face.

"Carter, it wasn't—" one of the men said, trying to explain why they were on the east wing, and no one was guarding the front door or Miamor's room as Carter had ordered.

Carter grabbed the man and pulled out his own gun, putting it in the man's mouth. "Open up, nigga!" Carter yelled as he harshly rubbed the barrel of the gun on the man's lips.

The man opened his mouth and put both of his hands up, not believing what was happening. The other henchmen just looked on in fear. They had never seen Carter lose his composure whatsoever, so to see him so irate was terrifying.

"I pay you niggas good to watch and protect my fortress, and look what you do. You niggas don't know how to make money. The only thing you have to do is stay on your post. I don't pay you niggas to stand around and play games. What the fuck? Anybody could have come in here and hurt my lady!" Carter yelled as he thought about how he could've crept past them without anyone knowing. "Who was supposed to be at the door?" he asked as he continued to grip the man by his collar. He glanced around looking for an answer, but no one said anything. "Who!" he asked again as he dug the gun deeper in the man's mouth.

The man he was holding raised his hand, unable to talk because the gun was in his mouth. Carter had found out all that he needed. He pulled the trigger, rocking him to sleep. Blood and noodles shot out the back of the man's head, and Carter released his grip, letting his body fall to the floor. He didn't even look at him fall. He just turned around and headed to check on Miamor. "Clean that shit up!" he yelled as he put his smoking gun on his hip. He had to send a message that he wasn't playing, and that's exactly what he did. Maybe if so much wasn't going on, he would not have gone that far. He wasn't the one for making regrets, so he whispered, "Don't fucking play with me!" to himself, as he climbed the stairs to get to Miamor.

When Carter walked in the room, he saw the nurse that he had hired sitting next to Miamor, half-asleep. She was an older black woman who seemed to be in her early fifties. He had hired her from a health care service just before he went to Haiti. Carter walked over to the nurse and placed his hand on her shoulder. "Hello, Mrs. Smith. You can leave now," he said as he greeted her with a smile and pulled out a wad of cash.

She smiled back and got up to retrieve her things.

Carter looked at Miamor, who was still in a comatose state. She never looked more beautiful in Carter's eyes. He bent over and kissed her on the head. "Hey, baby," he said as he smiled.

The nurse headed out of the door, and Carter remembered what he had just done downstairs, so he told her to exit out of the west wing's door. He didn't want her to see the gory scene that was downstairs by the main door.

She nodded her head in agreement, and exited the room, leaving him alone in the room with Miamor.

Carter sat at the edge of the bed and placed his hand on top of Miamor's. He would give anything for her to just open her eyes. He would pay for her to tell him that she loved him. He still didn't know who could do such a heinous act to such a beautiful girl. But when he found out who had done it, he would make them pay.

Never in his wildest dreams could he have guessed that her injuries were at the hands of his own flesh and blood, Mecca.

Carter was exhausted, and he was ready to go to sleep. He pulled up a chair so that he could fall asleep right next to Miamor, hoping that she would awaken. He grabbed a small blanket from the foot of the bed and positioned himself comfortably. He prepared to call it a night and closed his eyes. So much had been going on over the past week, and it had him drained. He said a quick prayer for his sister, Breeze, and whispered, "I love you."

Out of nowhere, Miamor, with a cracked and low voice, whispered, "I love you too," as she opened her eyes and let out a small grunt.

Carter quickly jumped up and looked into her eyes. He smiled. It felt so good to see her eyes after so long. "Oh my God, baby! You're up! I'm here. I got you," he said as he bent down and kissed her repeatedly on the forehead.

Miamor was so weak that she could barely keep her eyes open. They were so heavy that it felt like someone was pulling her eyelids down. She tried to move, but her body wasn't responding. It took all of her energy to whisper those three little words, "I love you," but those words were music to Carter's ears. He was so grateful, so happy.

"I thought I lost you, Miamor. I would have waited forever for you to wake up," Carter said as he felt his hands shaking. His nerves were getting the best of him because he was overwhelmed with joy. His queen was back.

Chapter Eleven

Miamor

"What are we going to do?" Anisa asked as she paced back and forth and stared at Murder's arrest on the TV.

"I don't know," I replied, clueless.

The police had Murder in handcuffs, and had confiscated the money he had on him; all the money he had to his name. His head hung low, and he tried to avoid the flash of the media cameras.

My stomach was doing somersaults as I watched in disbelief, and my foot tapped anxiously against the floor. I was pissed at Anisa, but I would never tell her. If she had not gone off on her ridiculous tangent, then none of this would have ever happened. No words needed to be spoken to establish guilt. We were both there, we knew how it had gone down, and she knew that it was her fault. In a zombie like state I walked past her. I was still covered in blood and needed to take a shower.

The eyes of the man that I had killed haunted me. I put the soiled clothing in a plastic bag and stepped under the hot stream of water. It was almost too hot to bear, but I needed it to cleanse myself. I was desperate for the shower to wash away the sins that I had committed that night. The blood ran down my body and turned pink as it swirled down the drain.

Why did this have to happen? I asked myself as my tears kicked in. I cried silently for all that I had lost. After everything that I had been through when I came out of lockup, my life finally felt normal. I had felt like I found a family in Murder and Anisa, but my disillusioned view of safety had come crashing down around me the moment I pulled my second trigger. Two lives had gone extinct behind my actions, and although I would never regret killing Perry, my second murder was weighing heavily on my heart. It was then that I realized I was not normal. I never had been, and after tonight, I never would be.

Scrubbing my skin until it was raw, I washed my body until the water ran cold. I was grateful for the film of steam that covered the bathroom mirror. I wasn't ready to face myself. I didn't want to look into my eyes, because I was sure that I would not recognize the girl who stared back at me.

Knock! Knock!

"Miamor, are you okay?" Anisa called through the door.

My hands shook as I picked up the plastic bag filled with my blood-soaked clothes, and I opened the door to let her in. "I'm fine," I answered. "I need to take these clothes to the incinerator."

She took my hand, reminding me of how she used to take care of me when we were little, then led me out of the apartment. We entered the room where the incinerator was and I tossed the bag inside. Anisa rubbed my hair and put her arms around me as we both watched it burn.

"Everything is going to be okay, Miamor. We have to move on, and you have to forget that tonight ever happened," Anisa said.

I looked at her with a blank expression. "What about Murder?"

Anisa didn't look at me. Instead, she stared into the fire. "Murder knew the risks of the game he was playing. I knew one day something would go down and he wouldn't come home. Today is that day."

I wanted to tell her that today would not have been "the day" if it hadn't been for her, but I had to take responsibility in the situation too, because I could have stopped it. "We have to help him get out of this, Nis," I protested.

"There is no getting out of this, Miamor. He got caught. I'm not going to risk you going away again. I can let him go, but I will never forgive myself if I have to see them take you away again. Murder is gone . . . it is what it is," she said coldly.

Murder ended up taking a plea. He got five to seven years on a weapons and tax evasion charge. They couldn't connect the body to him, because I had disposed of the gun, so that case went unsolved. I wanted to visit Murder, but Anisa thought it was best if we cut our ties and start fresh. Living life without Murder was easier said than done, however. Gone were the days of shopping sprees and lounging. Without him bringing in the paper, things got real tight for us. Anisa and I used up the money we'd gotten for her car in a matter of a couple months. Rent, groceries and bills ate that cash up quick. Murder's absence was felt almost immediately, because we realized all that he did for us, and now that he was gone. The ringing of the house phone was our only reminder that he was ever really there. We resulted to petty hustles; boosting clothes and petty credit card schemes just to get by, but still at the end of the month, dollars was short and we were on the verge of being thrown out on our asses.

"I'm not for being broke," Anisa stated seriously. "You might have to sell your car, Miamor."

I raised my eyebrows and looked at her like she was crazy. "Bitch, I'm not selling my whip. I'll sell some ass before I get rid of my car," I said adamantly.

Anisa burst into laughter as the ringing of the phone interrupted our conversation. "Well, we are going to have to think of something, because rent is due in a few days," she reminded me, the stress written all over her face.

The phone stopped ringing, and we sat in silence as we each searched for resolutions to our problems, but it wasn't long before it started again blaring in our ears.

"Fuck! I can't even think from that mu'fucka ringing all the damn time!" Anisa shouted.

"Why don't they just stop calling? I know they saw Murder's arrest in the papers and shit," I replied.

Anisa shook her head. "Nobody knew who Murder really was. To the rest of the world, he's just another nigga lost to the system. I'm the only person who knew about what he did. To everybody else, he was just a voice on the phone."

"How'd he collect his money?" I asked curiously.

"They'd wire the money to a Cayman account. Half up front, half after the job is done. Murder didn't trust anybody though. He always cleared the account after every job and stashed his dough in the safe."

Ring! Ring!

"Do you have access to the account?" I asked curiously.

"I had access to all of Murder's money, whether he knew it or not," Anisa smirked.

I shook my head and smirked. "Yo' slick ass!" I commented.

Ring! Ring!

My mind was spinning. My pockets were on empty and I was in desperate need of a dollar. My sister and I were three days off of being put out in the street. "Why don't we just answer it?" I asked.

"What?" Anisa said skeptically. She lowered her voice to a whisper as if we weren't in the apartment alone. "Miamor, I told you what type of business Murder was into . . ." Anisa said, but she stopped mid-sentence when she saw the look on my face. "Miamor, what the fuck are you thinking?" she asked, reading my mind.

"I'm just saying; we need money, and there is cash money on the other end of that receiver. All we got to do is pick it up," I said unsurely as I stood up and walked over to the phone.

Ring! Ring! Ring! Ring!

Anisa and I stared intensely at one another. We both knew that once I answered that line, there would be no turning back. She looked back at the table full of bills and then up at me. She nodded her head, and I lifted the phone to my ear. It was the day we accepted our first job, and the day the Murder Mamas was born.

Chapter Twelve

Miamor

Benjamin Wilkes aka Benny Dough was our first hit. I could never forget his name, because he was getting paper, and being flashy was what he lived to do. All of Brooklyn knew who he was. A big time party promoter in the city, he wasn't hard to find. We couldn't have asked for an easier mark. Like clockwork, on Sunday nights he frequented Tenders, a local strip joint. It was ballers' night, which attracted all the get-money niggas in the 'hood.

Anisa and I came out shining that night, whipping my Benz up to the club's valet as if we belonged amongst the 'hood's rich and infamous list. Rocking Gucci, diamonds, and Prada, to the naked eye we fit right in with Brooklyn's elite, but we knew the deal. We were fronting and dead broke, but we were about to put in work. Legs greased, body right, and hair and makeup on point, we slid into the club. Weed smoke was in the air and liquor flowed freely as we found a booth in the corner of the room. The small burner I had purchased from Murder's gun connect was underneath my dress, strapped to my inner thigh. We didn't have time to purchase another one, so we rolled with a single pistol, figuring that it would be all the muscle we would need to take care of the job.

Benny Dough was in the VIP section, popping bottles as he and his entourage made the club rain. They were being entertained by three strippers, and even I had to admit that they were some bad bitches. They each looked like they had been ripped straight from the pages of *King Magazine*. They were the type of bitches that regular chicks loved to hate, and they had his full attention as they danced seductively in front of him.

"We might have some competition," Anisa whispered in my ear.

I shook my head. "We're not trying to juice the nigga's pockets. We're here for a completely different reason. He's drunk, and they are the perfect distraction. Let them do what they do, and we'll do what we do," I replied. "Let's go to the bar. We can see better from over there."

Anisa and I made our way through the darkened club. Our hips commanding the attention of the patrons, the two of us together gained more interest than some of the dancers, but we kept it pushing. It was our first job, and neither of us wanted to fuck it up. Fifty thousand dollars was at stake, and we were about nothing but our paper that night.

"Can I get an apple martini?" I asked the bartender. I never took a sip from the drink, but I held it for good measure. I didn't want to be the only person at the bar without a glass in my hand. I wanted to blend in while I discreetly watched every move that Benny made. I watched Anisa kill her drink, and I could see that she was nervous, but the liquid courage she'd just consumed would be more than enough to get her through the night. We both prayed that everything went perfectly. We were a far cry from the seasoned killer that Murder was, but we were stepping into his shoes. I crossed my fingers and hoped that things played out right.

I was so focused that I didn't even notice the dude that had slid into the seat next to me. He turned the swivel stool I was sitting in around so that I was facing him. I frowned, and was about to say something until he leaned into my ear.

"You and yo' girl about to rob that nigga or something?" he asked.

His question caught me completely off guard, and my heartbeat began to speed up. *Are we that obvious?* I thought as I gave him the evil eye and stood to leave.

Dude grabbed my arm gently and pulled me near him. "I respect your hustle, ma. It's sexy as long as I don't come into your crosshairs, nah mean?" his BK accent was strong, and his Usher cologne invaded my space while his dark bedroom eyes scanned me from head to toe.

"I don't know what you're talking about," I responded shortly as I titled my head to the side and looked up at him. He smiled; I didn't.

Any other day I might have listened to what he was kicking. The presidential on his wrist indicated that he was worth my time, but I wasn't there for all that. I really wished the nigga would get out of my space so that I could re-focus, but he wasn't moving. I looked over at Anisa, who was still on point. Benny Dough had never left her eyesight. I turned back around to the man in front of me. "Did you want something?" I asked him.

"What's your name?" he asked.

"Nigga, what's your name?" I countered.

He laughed and rubbed the hairs of his full beard. "Joell," he responded. "I own this club."

I clapped my hands sarcastically and said, "Congratulations! That must impress a lot of women." I rolled my eyes, hoping that the nigga would take a hint and get lost, but again, he didn't.

"I just thought I'd tip your hand a little bit and let you know that all eyes are on you. You walk into my strip joint looking good, smelling good . . . got these niggas watching you more than they watching my dancers, but you got your sights on one nigga. He looks like a mark to me. Somebody like you shouldn't have to rob and steal to eat, Ms. Lady. You could be very well taken care of," he said.

"I'm not putting on no show, and I don't know nothing about all that you talking. We're just here for the entertainment," I replied without looking at him. My eyes found Benny Dough, and noticed that he was preparing to leave. He wasn't sloppy drunk, but I could tell that he was tipsy. I nudged Anisa and grabbed my clutch. "It was nice to meet you, Joell. You have a good evening," I said with a curt smile.

He leaned back against the bar and watched me walk away. I put an extra switch in my hips just to show him something that he would never get, and walked right past Benny Dough out of the club.

As soon as Anisa and I claimed our car from valet parking, we changed clothes inside, removed our makeup and put on jeans and sneakers. Arab scarves were tied around our necks. We waited patiently, and minutes later, Benny Dough came out of the club with the stripper chicks and two other men following behind him. We were silent and breathing hard in anticipation as we followed him and his entourage to a cheap motel. They were two cars deep, so we made sure that we didn't tail them too closely. The last thing we needed was for them to get suspicious.

"There are six of them and two of us. You know all of them niggas is strapped. How are we gon' pull this off now?" Anisa asked.

"We wait," I said. I wasn't exactly sure how we would pull it off either. We were outnumbered and outgunned, but we really didn't have a choice. We were already paid half up front. We had to come through on our end, so it was all or nothing. We watched the room for a half an hour, and suddenly the door opened. One of the guys came out. Anisa went to get out of the car.

"What are you doing?" I whispered harshly as she got out and waved the dude over.

"Hey! I'm sorry to bother you," she said as she walked toward the guy. "Me and my girl are having some car trouble. It won't start. Can you help us please?" she asked.

This was not a part of the plan, and butterflies fluttered in my stomach. *What is she doing? Now this nigga done seen her face and everything!* I thought heatedly.

The nigga was a sucker for a pretty face, because he came right over without question and tapped the front of the car. "Open the hood," he instructed. I did as I was told and then hit the release button for the trunk as well. I saw him lean over to check out the engine, so I grabbed the gun, and got out of the car.

"Show me your hands," I said as I raised the gun to his head. Surprise swept over his face and he opened his mouth to speak. "If you want to live to see tomorrow, then you'll shut the fuck up," I said calmly. The look on his face told me that he was fuming. "Yeah, you fell for the okey doke," I commented, further pissing him off.

Anisa reached into his waistline and relieved him of his cell phone, the hotel room key, and a black .45. "Thank you," she sang as she released the safety and cocked it back.

With steel pressed to both sides of his head, the dude became much more humble. "I got a daughter, man!" he pleaded. "I don't know what y'all bitches want, but you can have it. My whip, money, whatever."

We didn't respond, but we took that nigga for a walk to the back of the car. I lifted the trunk. We were moving in sync as if we had been doing this for years. She was the Thelma to my Louise. "Get in," Anisa ordered.

The dude reluctantly climbed inside, and we closed the trunk. After making sure that he was locked inside, I turned to her with big eyes and whispered, "What the fuck was that, Nis? You've got to warn me before you make a play like that! The nigga saw our faces and everything," I fussed.

"So, we'll pop his ass so that he ain't telling nothing," she responded as she pulled her scarf over her face. I did the same. The only thing that could be seen was our hair and our eyes as we made our way to the door. I put my finger to my lips and then put my ear to the door. The sounds of music could be heard.

Anisa inserted the key slowly, and when the locked released, I rushed inside. "Everybody on the floor! If I have to say it more than once, I'ma leave you stinkin' in this bitch!" I yelled as Anisa and I pointed our guns around the room.

"What the fuck? Do you bitches know who the fuck you're fucking with?" one of the guys asked.

Boom!

He fell dead where he stood. I was surprised that Anisa had shot him, but I didn't show it. I barely even flinched, because I knew in order to stay in control, I'd have to keep my composure. "Now, does anybody else have any more questions?" I asked. "Sit on your hands!" I demanded.

"There's a nigga—" one of the girls began to speak, but I smacked the shit out of her with the gun.

"Didn't I tell you to shut the fuck up?" I asked. I could see the larceny in her eyes, but I didn't come there for her, so I kept it moving.

We took the zip ties out of our pockets and began to bind everybody by their hands and feet, but before we could get to the last girl, a nigga came bursting out of the bathroom. He rushed me and at the exact same moment Benny Dough tackled Anisa.

Boom! Boom!

I heard two gunshots go off, and then heard Anisa groaning as I struggled against the dude as we both tried to get a good hold on the gun. He was using his weight as an advantage and had me pinned to the floor, but I was holding on to the gun for dear life. I couldn't get to the trigger. He smacked fire from my ass, causing the entire right side of my face to burn and stars to appear before my eyes. I knew it was over when I found myself looking down the barrel of the gun.

"Yeah, bitch! Where's all that mouth now?" he asked.

I closed my eyes and prepared for the worst. I didn't want to see the bullets that ended my life. I inhaled deeply, gulping in the last bit of air that my lungs would ever taste.

Boom! Boom! Boom!

The gunshots deafened my ears, but when I didn't feel any pain, I opened my eyes. I scrambled backwards until my back hit the wall as I watched the dude fall to his knees as three bloodstains began to spread through the front of his shirt. I expected to see Anisa holding the smoking gun, but instead, one of the strippers had shot him.

"Anisa!" I yelled as I crawled over to her. Her neck was raw from being choked, and she was covered in blood. "Anisa . . . where are you hit?" I asked as my hands roamed her body.

She coughed and gulped in air. "It's not mine, Miamor . . . I'm good."

I helped her to her feet and retrieved our guns.

The girl who had saved me was cutting the ties from her friends' hands.

"Thanks," I said as I looked her in the eye. I had every intention of killing them when I came into the room, but after what she had done, I knew that I couldn't go through with it.

"I hope you bitches don't think that y'all are getting what's in they pockets. This was our lick in the first place," the girl I had smacked spoke up. "I tried to tell your ass there was a nigga in the bathroom," she said as she rubbed the side of her face and ice-grilled me. "Now you mu'fuckas done fucked up our money. We won't be able to get back to the nigga house to hit the safe. It was a hundred thousand in that bitch."

"One-hundred-thousand dollars?" Anisa asked.

"Yeah, bitch, a hunnid stacks," the girl shot back.

"If we can take you to the safe, we split the money five ways," Anisa said.

"Bitch, you killed everybody who knew the combo! Crazy ass bitches!" the same girl yelled.

"Bitch, I ain't gone be too many more of your bitches," I said seriously. "Now, can we discuss this somewhere else, before the police come in here and arrest all of us?"

I took a pillowcase off of the bed and tossed my gun inside. I then held it out for the three girls. I knew they were strapped, because the one who had helped me had pulled her gun from nowhere. "We don't know y'all like that. As long as we talking about getting this money, ain't nobody carrying burners," I said. Each of the three girls put their guns inside, and then Anisa followed suit. They reluctantly followed us to our car.

The guy in the trunk kicked and screamed when he heard us start the car. The three girls were in the backseat.

"What the fuck type of shit is y'all into? Y'all got niggas in the trunk?" one of them asked. I looked at them in the rearview, but didn't respond. We were all silent as we drove to a twenty-four-hour diner, where we came to some type of agreement regarding the money in the safe. Anisa and I didn't say anything about what we had been paid to do. They didn't need to know all of that. We just wanted our piece of their pie.

Robyn was the leader of their clique it seemed, and also the one I had smacked. Beatrice was a dark-skinned, weave wearing ghetto chick. I couldn't read the two of them very well at first, but I was instantly endeared to the third girl, Aries. She was the one who had saved my life that night.

After getting to know one another, we led the girls back out to the deserted parking lot. It was the middle of the night and there was no one around, so we popped the trunk. We all burst out laughing when we saw the dude curled up like a bitch. He was so scared that he had pissed on himself.

"Damn! Me can't believe me was actually going to give chu some," Aries stated.

We all pulled our guns back out of the pillowcase since a low level of trust had been established. Aries pointed her gun at the dude. "Get chu bitch ass out de trunk," she said. The dude climbed out and stared at the five of us standing around him with pistols in our hand. "Chu going to lead us to Benny Dough's house, and chu going to help us crack de safe," Aries instructed.

The guy didn't respond, so Anisa cocked her gun, putting one in the chamber and pointed it at him. "Get in the car."

Twenty minutes later, we were pulling up to a two story suburban home. "Who else lives here?" I asked.

"Nobody," the dude responded wearily.

I turned around to look him in the eye. I knew he was afraid. I could hear the fear in his voice. "Remember that daughter you were talking about earlier. Don't be stupid. We just want the money," I explained.

He nodded his head and then led us into the house. The guy reached under a flowerpot and grabbed the spare key, then opened the door. He had five bitches with attitudes on his ass, so he knew not to make a bad move. He led the way up the stairs to one of the bedrooms, then removed a painting from the wall.

"What's the combo?" Beatrice asked.

"I don't know the combination to that man's safe," the guy protested.

I knew he was lying when he said it, so I shot him without hesitation. I was tired of playing games.

"Aghh!" he screamed in agony as he dropped to the floor and held onto his bleeding foot.

"If you want to keep the other one, start talking," I instructed.

"Ha! Bitch, you really are crazy as hell!" Beatrice laughed out in amusement as she watched the dude hold his foot and cry in excruciation. "I'd fuck with her all day! That bitch ain't scared to do shit!" she said, meaning it as a compliment.

"Thirty-four, twenty-three, ten!" he yelled. "Fuck!" His screams of pain echoed throughout the house.

Anisa tried the set of numbers and smiled as she opened the safe. "Oh shit!" she exclaimed. "This looks like more than a hundred thou."

As soon as I saw the money stacks sitting in the safe, I pulled the trigger on that nigga. He had seen my face, and there was no way I could send him home to his daughter in any other way except for in a box. To my surprise, he got hit with three more bullets as well, because as soon as I withdrew, so did Aries, Beatrice, and Robyn. We filled him with lead, filled our pockets with paper, and disappeared into the night.

We all headed back to my apartment, where we decided we wouldn't spend any money until we heard what the streets would say about the murders. Since we didn't know one another, we all wanted to be in each other's presence to make sure nobody fucked up and got loose lips.

Chapter Thirteen

Miamor

I woke up early the next day and maneuvered silently throughout the apartment. I didn't want to wake Anisa or the new tagalong bitches we had picked up the night before. I didn't know Robyn, Aries, and Beatrice, but I was grateful that they were there. *Things could have gone real bad for us last night,* I thought as I shuddered at the thought of how close I had come to death. If it had not been for them, Anisa and I would have both been taking dirt naps, despite that fact I still did not trust them. Respect them, yes . . . trust them, hell no!

I thought that my heart would be full of dread, but strangely, my conscience wasn't phased by what I had done the night before. It was like the higher my body count rose, the less it affected me. I was choosing to become a killer. I had made the decision to pick up where Murder left off, all in the pursuit of the American dream, and there was no turning back. *It's just business,* I told myself as I made my way to my car.

My black skinny jeans looked as if they were painted on, and the white Marc Jacobs blouse revealed my cleavage and jewels. The white peep-toe Prada heels I wore completed my outfit as I climbed into my car and peeled out of the parking lot. I didn't tell anyone where I was going, not even Anisa. I knew she'd hit the roof if I told her I was going to see Murder, but I had to check on him. Plus, I thought he deserved a cut of the money we'd made last night. I promised myself that I would keep money on his commissary and put the rest of his cut aside until he got out.

I couldn't understand how it was so easy for Anisa to move on and just forget about all that Murder had done for her, because in the short year that I had known him, he would always be a part of me. I had feelings for him. If it wasn't for him, I would have been locked up. Instead, he took the heat, and I felt fucked up because I was just getting around to visiting him. My bone-straight wrap and Chinese bangs ruffled as the wind whipped through my hair. I hoped I wasn't making the trip for nothing. I didn't even know if I was listed on his visitor's log, but it was a chance I was willing to take.

I hit a department store first and picked up items that I thought Murder might need; a small care package that could hold him over for a while. Then taking the BQE toward Queens, I exited at Astoria Boulevard, then followed the city blocks until I hit Hazen Street. When I arrived at Riker's parking lot, I stepped out of the car with the box of personal items in my hands as I made my way to the bus that was traveling over the bridge to the facility.

As soon as I stepped foot on the bus, I knew it was going to be a miserable trip. There were babies crying, ghetto baby mamas arguing and talking cash shit, and tired wives who had done this routine time and time again. I shook my head, knowing that I could never be one of the chicks waiting on the outside. I had done years of lockup on my own as a child. I wasn't trying to do five more waiting on Murder or anybody else. It was then that I knew that I could not ride out Murder's sentence with him. When a loved one is locked up, that time affects the inmate and everyone around him.

As I looked at an older woman with a wedding band on her finger, I couldn't help but ask, "Are you here to see your husband?"

My question caught her off guard, but she shook her head and answered, "No, baby. I'm here for that knucklehead son of mine. He grew up watching me make this same trip to come and see his father, and now he's landed himself in the same predicament . . . behind the white man's walls. Like father like son, I guess."

The sadness in her eyes scared me, and I fidgeted uncomfortably in my seat as I noticed the lifelessness in the woman. She had no hope, no light in her eye. *That'll never be me,* I thought as uneasiness filled my stomach. As much as I cared for Murder, I knew that after today I would not come back. *The best I can do is letters and make sure his money is right,* I thought. I knew it was selfish, but it was real. The truth of the matter was, Murder was not my man, even though somewhere deep inside I wished that he had been.

After practically being molested by the guards and storing my personal items in a locker, I was finally escorted into a waiting room. I sat at the small table, growing more nervous as each minute ticked by. My manicured hand tapped impatiently, as butterflies filled my stomach. I was in the middle of a prison, but I felt as if I was going on a blind date. I rubbed my sweaty hands on my jeans, and then finally Murder came waltzing into view. His swagger was still so on point. Even in the jail hookup he had on he possessed an aura of respect. I smiled as he came near me.

"Hey, Murder!" I greeted as I stood to hug him.

He held me extra tight and extra close.

"My li'l mama!" he whispered, "Thanks for coming."

"I'm sorry it took me so long. It's been rough. I had to let things die down, you know?"

Murder nodded his head, then motioned for me to take a seat. "I know," he answered. "Where's your sister?" His eyebrows dipped low when he mentioned Anisa, as if he already knew the answer to his own question.

"Um, she couldn't make it, Murder. She told me to tell you—" I was about to make up an excuse on her behalf, but Murder waved his hand in dismissal.

"Don't do that, ma. You've never lied to me before. Don't start now because of your sister. I know Anisa. A nigga can't keep her when he's down; only when he at the top. I don't want to talk about her," he said with a hint of sadness in his voice. He touched my chin, making me smile. "You're here. Let's talk about that. Why did *you* come?"

His question had me stuck. *Why did I come?* I asked myself. I looked him directly in the eyes.

The chemistry between our gaze was magnetic. "I owe you," I said.

"That's it?" he countered with a boyish charm.

"I was worried about you."

"Uh-huh," he responded. "You sure that's it?"

I hesitated before I continued, but knew that I wasn't being honest with myself. "I care about you, Murder."

"It's a little bit deeper than that, li'l mama, but I'll play by your rules. I care about you too, ma. Always have . . . always will," he said as he grabbed my hand.

My heart was beating out of my chest. "I'm sorry. I feel like it's my fault you're in here."

"This ain't on you. These walls ain't shit to me. In five years, I'ma walk out the same mu'fucka," he said as he kissed the inside of my wrist.

Seeing him in good spirits felt good. The interaction between us felt so natural . . . so right. He was my nigga, first and foremost. Murder and I were friends, but the fact that my attraction to him was growing by the second had me thinking about waiting for him; had me wanting to be there for him for those long five years.

"Murder, Anisa will never understand this. She's my sister, and I can't pick you over her, no matter how much I'm feeling you," I told him.

He nodded his head in understanding. "I know, Miamor. I would never ask you to. I know the type of woman you are. You're loyal, and that's one of the reasons why I feel the way I do about you. Like I told you before, it's not meant to be for us, but it don't stop me from wanting you. In five years, I'ma look you up, believe that, ma. You're my li'l mama always. Life moves on, and I would never ask you to wait or to hurt your sister. I'ma come check for you when I'm free though."

I smiled and pulled my hand away from Murder's. "I have one more thing to tell you," I said. He was silent as he waited for me to continue. "I answered your phone," I said. My words hit him like a ton of bricks, and his face collapsed into a mixture of sorrow and anger. "I'm on that now. Every time, I'll have your paper put aside for you and I'll keep your books on full in here. When you get out, you'll have money waiting on you."

Murder put his face in his hands and shook his head from side to side. "I didn't want that for you, Miamor. That's not for you. You deserve better than that."

I stood to my feet and wiped the tears from my eyes. "I don't think a better life is in the cards for me," I whispered.

Murder stood and pulled me close, putting his hands in my back jean pockets as we hugged. He pulled a picture out of my pocket. "What's this?" he asked.

I had meant to give it to him when I first arrived. It was a picture of us together on my birthday, holding up bottles of champagne.

He pulled me near him one more time and whispered in my ear. "Be careful. Never think twice about pulling a trigger. Turn your heart cold, Miamor. Think like a nigga, because acting like a bitch will get you killed. It's the only way you'll make it. Slump a nigga before he can slump you. No body, no weapon—"

"No murder," I whispered, finishing his sentence, our lips so close together that they touched when I spoke the words.

He pulled back and looked me in the eye. "You've already done your first job," he said in surprise.

I nodded my head, stood on my tip toes and kissed his cheek. "Good bye, Murder."

He held onto my hand as I walked away, until the distance finally separated us. "Holla at me, Miamor . . . at least once a month to let me know you're okay!" he yelled after me.

I nodded my head in agreement, and then walked out of his life.

When I returned to the apartment, the atmosphere was tense. Everyone was silent and staring at me in suspicion as soon as I set foot inside the door.

"Where the fuck have you been?" Robyn asked.

I looked at her like she was crazy, and bypassed her without responding as I went into my room. The silly bitch obviously didn't know about me, because if she did, she would have known that I would smack fire from her ass for talking to me out the side of her neck.

She followed behind me. "Look, you're the one who said we should lay low and let the streets cool down before we get to spending money, then when we wake, up you're ghost," she said. "What are we supposed to think?"

"I don't really give a damn what you think. I had to handle something, that's all you need to know," I replied.

The girls made their way into my room, and Anisa stood by the door. I could feel her staring at me. I knew she wanted to know where I had disappeared to so early in the morning, but I wasn't telling. Nobody needed to know. Where I went was my business. Fuck all them hoes!

"Well, I've been thinking," Beatrice stated as she sat on my bed and looked around at everyone in the room. "Y'all didn't even know about the money in the safe before we told you, so that means y'all were there for something else. We want in."

"Want in?" Anisa repeated.

"Yeah, whatever y'all got going on, we want in. There is only two of y'all. Without us, things could have turned out different for y'all last night. I don't know what exactly y'all do, but I know this plush condo and that Benzo you driving don't come cheap. We want in," Beatrice asserted.

Anisa and I looked at each other with raised eyebrows, and as if on cue, the phone began to ring.

Ring! Ring!

I was skeptical at first, but I knew that having more chicks on our team could be a good thing. Our chances of being caught slipping would decrease drastically if we hooked up with Robyn, Aries, and Beatrice.

Ring! Ring!

"A'ight," I said. "We're not into the petty robbery game though."

"We don't give a fuck what you into it. If it's about money, then we're with it," Robyn spoke up confidently.

Ring! Ring!

"We'll see," I replied as I stood up and rushed to pick up the phone, with them hot on my trail. I took down the details of the call and turned around to face the group.

"You want in?" I asked.

"We want in," Aries reiterated impatiently.

I handed her a piece of paper that had the name of our next hit on it. "Murder that nigga. It needs to be done quickly and quietly," I instructed, and then walked away, leaving them to their thoughts.

Anisa followed behind me, and once we were in my room alone, she closed the door. "Are you crazy!" she asked.

"They want in, so let them prove that they can handle it. If they fuck up, we will handle them," I responded. "Just relax."

The next day, I received a text message from a number I didn't recognize: WATCH THE NEWS! I frowned when I read the words, but went into Anisa's room and told her to turn the channel:

"*. . . This is Allison Fisher, reporting for WWOR. Gun violence has once again taken a hold of the Bronx. Thaddeus Johnson was gunned down in his vehicle today* *on East 142nd Street. Witnesses say that two unidentified females were riding a red motorcycle, when they pulled up to a traffic light next to Mr. Johnson's car and opened fire. This young woman was the passenger in Mr. Johnson's car when the shooting took place. "Can you tell us what you saw?" the reporter asked.*

The girl's voice shook as she replied, "It all just happened so fast. All I remember is listening to the music one second, and hearing loud gunshots the next. I was ducked down in my seat. I was too afraid to look up. There was so much blood. I thought that I would die. I can't believe this happened . . ."

Anisa and I watched the newscast in shock. The girl who was being interviewed was Robyn, and the guy that had been killed was the hit I had given them. Anisa chuckled and said, "She deserves an Oscar for that performance."

"They pulled it off!" I whispered in disbelief as I sat back against the headboard on Anisa's bed. Anisa looked at me and shook her head from side to side. My cell phone rang, and an unknown number popped up. "Hello?" I answered.

"So, we're in?" I instantly recognized Aries' distinctive accent.

"You're in," I replied with a smile. The average type of chick would not have been able to pull off what the three of them had. They were ruthless and conniving. They were just like me, and now they were on my team.

Chapter Fourteen

Miamor

A year passed, and life was good! Anisa, Beatrice, Robyn, Aries and I were lying in the sun on a cruise ship just off the coast of Miami. We had planned that particular trip to celebrate our success. After Anisa and I got to know the other girls, we knew that they could be very helpful in our newfound profession. Before I even knew it, we established the Murder Mamas. At first it was a little joke, but the name was fitting and sort of stuck. We all even got "Murder Mama" tattooed on ourselves to show our allegiance.

It did not take long for niggas to catch wind of us. We had expanded and took jobs from Jersey, Philly, and even D.C. The word spread quickly in the streets, because our phone constantly rang for new jobs. We only took jobs by referral, meaning you would have to know someone that hired us before to even have a conversation with us about our services. We had a secret society, and the only thing we asked for was trust. We sometimes set up clowns that were stunting too hard and robbed them, but we only did that when we traveled out of town. Our main hustle was murder-for-hire. That's what paid the bills.

The one thing about killing is; just like everything else you do, the more you do it, the better you get. I believe my heart had grown the coldest of our whole crew. I never thought twice about a murder once it was done. The only thing I thought about was the payoff. Some might call it cold-blooded, but I call it just being Miamor.

We all sat, sipping our exotic drinks and enjoying the sun. I looked over at Beatrice, who lay out on the deck with her big Gucci shades on and smiled. "Bitch, you know you don't need any more sun," I joked, referring to her dark ebony skin tone. We all burst into laughter, knowing she was the darkest of the crew.

Beatrice held up her middle finger without saying a word as she smiled and continued to sip her Long Island iced tea. She is what you called "ghetto fabulous." She originally was from BX, and I loved her style. She always told it how it was, and had a tendency to be loud at the wrong times. But it was what it was; she was my girl . . . real bitch.

Robyn was kind of sneaky in my eyes, but I dealt with her because she was resourceful. Her ass was like the sibling that you loved because you had to. She was my sister, but I could not stand her ass sometimes. She was a little older than me, about Anisa's age, and she knew every hustler in every borough. Don't ask me how, but she always knew who was coming up on the streets and who was next in line to be "the man." That was useful for us when we occasionally robbed niggas. But we did have one golden rule—never rob or take a hit on anyone we encountered before. It would be too much of a risk for us.

Aries was a sweetheart. She had a heavy Barbados accent, and it was hard to understand her at times, but I managed. She was petite, with beautiful shoulder-length twists in her hair that fit her exotic personality perfectly. She was one year younger than me, and kind of quiet. But don't let that fool you. Aries was a killer. I noticed that she didn't hesitate to kill if the money was right. She was the closest person to me, besides Anisa, because we were just alike. She was an asset to the squad for sure.

We all enjoyed the sunrays and sounds of the churning waves as we relaxed and conversed. In the midst of our conversation, the phone rang. We all sat up, recognizing that particular ring. I had all the calls from Murder's line forwarded to a cell phone used only for our hits. I put my finger over my lips to signal the girls to be quiet before I picked up. They all stared at me as I flipped up the phone and placed it to my ear. I remained silent and just listened.

"I have a job that requires your services. I want you to listen, and listen very closely," a man said with a deep Russian accent. He continued, "I have a problem that needs to be resolved. I want this done within thirty days. The contract is worth one-hundred-thousand-dollars. Half will be given up front, and the rest will be paid upon completion. You can find the information on the target in locker number 1356 at the Grand Central train terminal, and you can find the key under the station's bench, eight rows down."

I quickly reached into my purse and grabbed a pen and a small piece of paper to jot down the information. I just listened and wondered what type of job this was. I never had someone come so organized, and also we mainly only dealt with 'hood niggas. This was far from a 'hood guy" that we were used to handling business with. He paused, and there was a brief moment of silence on the phone before he continued.

"I take it that you want the job, since you haven't hung up," the Russian said before he let out a small chuckle. "Very well then. The money will be placed in a bag in the locker along with the information. Good day," he said before he left me with the dial tone.

I slowly closed down the phone and looked at my girls, who were all staring at me, anxiously waiting to see who had called.

"Well what did he say?" Anisa asked as she threw her hands up.

I took my time before I spoke, almost too excited to let the words come out of my mouth. "One . . . hundred . . . stacks!" I said as I jumped up and watched as my girls cheered and slapped hands. This was the payday we were looking for. That was about $20,000 apiece. Usually we would have to split $50,000 for one hit. Twenty to ourselves sounded real good. It was the last day of the cruise, and we were all eager to get back to NY to get that money . . . the Murder Mama way.

We sat in our condo in midtown Manhattan. We all moved in with each other a couple of months back. We didn't want to live in the 'hood, now that our operation was booming. Everyone sat and waited patiently for Anisa to return. She went to the station to retrieve the money and information. She told us that she wanted to go alone, just in case it was a setup by police, considering that we had never done business with this mysterious Russian guy before. She said there was no reason for all of us to do down. "Do you think it's legit?" Beatrice asked as she split open a blunt and began to fill it with kush weed. That girl knew she loved her weed. She was a bigger weed head then me, and I had learned from the best, being that Murder and I had shared at least three blunts a day before he was arrested. "I don't know. I hope so," I responded as I looked down at my watch. "Where is she? She should be back by now," I said, noticing that she had been gone longer than expected. Just as the negative feelings began to invade my thoughts, Anisa came through the door with a duffel bag and a big manila folder. "What took you so damn long?" I asked as I stood up. "I had to think about if I should take the money or not," she answered. All of us grew confused looks on our face.

"What chu mean?" Aries asked as she put her hands on her hips. Obviously, she already had plans for her share of the money, as we all did.

"Look at this," Anisa said as she threw the folder on the coffee table.

I picked up the folder, and when I saw the face of the man in the pictures, I quickly understood what Anisa meant.

"Fuck!' Beatrice said as she looked at the picture along with me. It was Joell, the owner of the club, Tenders, and also Robyn, Aries, and Beatrice's former boss. Taking this job would be breaking our golden rule: never hit someone we know or had ever encountered before.

"Me no believe dis' shit!" Aries exclaimed as she flopped down on the couch and put her hands on her head.

"He used to be our boss! He knows us!" Beatrice exclaimed. "We can't hit anybody we know, remember!" she said in total frustration.

"Fuck that! I'm about to get this money, with or without y'all. Me and Miamor don't know this nigga," Anisa exclaimed.

I remembered encountering Joell back at the strip club a while ago, but I remained silent, because I wasn't ready to give up on that money just yet. "Just hold up a minute. We are talking about one-hundred-thousand-dollars, ladies," I said, trying to weigh our options.

"You said it was a Russian guy on the phone, right?" Beatrice asked as she squinted her eyes, letting us know she was thinking hard about the task at hand.

"Yeah," I responded.

"I remember one time at the club, two Russian men burst in and put a gun to Joell's head in front of the whole club. Remember that, Robyn?" Beatrice asked.

"Yeah, I remember that shit. They were yelling about him owing them some money. You know Joell got that gambling bug bad," Robyn stated.

"That's the reason why they are at his ass," I added, as things started to make more sense. "I know we said we can't hit anybody that we know, but think about it. This is a lot of money. It is enough to move out of this grimy city. Miami looked real good this past weekend, ladies. Think about living near an ocean and not having to worry about karma catching up with us. If we stay in New York, we will always have to look over our shoulders. This is our way out," I said as I grabbed the duffel bag from Anisa's shoulder and dumped the stacks of money on the coffee table. Everyone's eyes were glued to the money, and it provided a sort of adrenaline rush for everyone. We were all paper chasers, and at that moment, I knew they would be down to kill Joell. The looks in their eyes told it all.

Anisa and I looked at each other and smiled, knowing that they were game. If they weren't, then Anisa and I would have done it by our damn selves, I'm sure of that.

It seemed as if all the tension left the room and everyone had small smirks on their faces. We were about to put a plan in motion.

***

Three weeks passed, and we were in the perfect position to take care of Joell. Everything was going as planned. Come to find out, Joell was sweet on Beatrice, but she never gave him any play. I told her to approach him as if she had a change of heart, so we could get close to him. I told her she would have to give up the pussy, and it was all in the game. Beatrice was smart, and she always lived by money over everything, so she wasn't hard to convince. Her deep chocolate skin, slim waist and extraordinarily large ass was eye candy to any man, so when she presented that to a sex fiend like Joell, he took the bait with no problem. Joell was a hard man to hit, I must admit. He knew there was a contract on his head, so he moved accordingly. He never went anywhere without his goons. Even when he met Beatrice at a hotel, he had two goons standing outside waiting for him. This hit was far more difficult than any of us imagined, but we were not called the best for nothing.

Beatrice spent every day with him for weeks, softening him up for the inevitable. She eventually convinced him to take her to Connecticut for a weekend at the world famous Clearwater Hotel and Spa, without his goons. I don't know how she did it, but she got him to do it. I guess she was putting it on him in the bedroom to get him to step out of his square. However, she did it, I didn't care. The only thing I knew was that we were about to be one-hundred-thousand-dollars richer.

I pulled into the luxurious spa parking lot alone. I arrived there six hours before Beatrice and Joell were scheduled to get there. I wanted to get there early and scope the scene, preparing myself for the hit. I got out and checked myself into the hotel. I carried my Gucci luggage to the front entrance and walked with a model's precision across the immaculate marble floor that made up the hotel's lobby. I wore a blonde wig and big shades, trying to avoid the chances of me being identified on camera. I checked in under an alias with the help of my fake ID and credit card. I told the other girls to stay home and let me do this one on my own. I didn't want all of them to come to the spa. It would only draw more attention to us. Too many black mu'fuckas in Connecticut was sure to raise somebody's red flag. Only Beatrice and I were going to complete this job, and would return to them once it was over.

Anisa and I argued over who would be the one to actually go with B to do the hit. She didn't want me to go without her, but we all agreed that I was the most ruthless of the crew, and she had to fall back. I assured her that Beatrice and I could handle it. B was going to ride up there with Joell, and I would kill him later that night while he was naked on a masseuse table.

Make it quick. In five minutes, come in. The door will be unlocked.

I looked at Beatrice's text on my cell phone and took a deep breath as I prepared myself mentally, focusing on the goal at the end of it all . . . money. Beatrice and I had gone over this plan the previous night at least fifty times, and we both knew the drill. First, she was going to get him drunk and relaxed. Then, she was going to offer an erotic massage on a masseuse table, naked of course, so he wouldn't have access to his gun that he kept on him at all times. I would sneak in and hit him with two hollow points to the back of the head. "In and out, like a robbery," as we would say. He would never see it coming; rock his ass to sleep . . . *Cha-ching*!

I looked at the clock, and it was a couple of strokes past ten p.m. My heart no longer beat rapidly before I killed someone. Repetition had taken away all of my insecurities when it came to my murder game. I looked at murder as if it was a job, not a sin. I went about killing just as a doctor would go about performing surgery, with expertise and precision. I was meticulous about every detail and never allowed my nerves to rattle me.

I carefully placed the bullets in the clip of my small .25 caliber pistol. I wore gloves to avoid the possibility of leaving any prints on the bullets. I had music playing in the background to get me in my mood, and bobbed my head to the rhythm while loading the gun. After I was locked and loaded, I removed my gloves and put them, along with the gun inside my purse. I had on a black business suit, the blond wig, and my stilettos on. My life wasn't a damn movie. You couldn't wear all black—mask and gloves—when you went to murk someone. You have to blend in, so people wouldn't look at you twice when you're leaving the scene. So I looked into the mirror and gave myself a once over before I exited the room. I had already put my bags in the car, and Beatrice and I were planning to make a quick getaway after the dirt was done.

I slowly walked out of the room and closed the door on my way to the top floor where Beatrice and Joell were. I then removed my gloves from my purse and stuffed them into my pocket as I headed toward the elevator. While on the elevator, I avoided facing the camera, turning my back to it as I pulled out my phone. First, I texted Beatrice and confirmed that I was on my way up, and then I dialed Anisa's number. I surprisingly had service on the elevator.

"Hello," Anisa said as she picked up the phone.

"Okay, I'm about to take care of it now. I love you," I said to her just as I always did before we took care of business.

"I love you too," she said back to me.

With that, the bell rang, signaling that I had reached my floor. I hung up the phone and walked out of the elevator. I reached the room, and just as promised, the door was slightly open and ready for me to sneak in. When I stepped in, I heard smooth jazz playing and the sounds of running water as I crossed the threshold of the door. The aroma of lavender scented candles danced in the air as the flickering candle lights illuminated the spacious presidential suite. My girl had set it up so nice for me. Beatrice was always on point like that. The lights were low, just like I anticipated. He would never see it coming. The room was so dark that I could barely see anything. The steam from the hot tub had it all foggy inside. I stepped a couple of feet in and I pulled out my gun, expecting to see Beatrice rubbing down Joell, but before I could even react, I felt a strong arm grab me from behind, and then I felt the cold steel of a gun pressed to my head.

The lights came on, and what I saw would be sketched in my mind forever. Beatrice was tied to the chair with blood running down her neck. She had been cut from ear to ear, and her eyes were staring aimlessly. She was dead. I then saw Joell smiling as he held a bloody knife, alongside three of his goons. The goon that had me at gunpoint quickly relieved me of my weapon and gripped me tightly from behind, placing me in a tight chokehold.

"Well, well, well! We have been waiting on you," Joell said as he reached into his pocket and pulled out Beatrice's cell phone and looked at it. He obviously saw the texts that I had sent her the whole time.

I had walked straight into a trap. I was speechless. The sight of Beatrice's bloody body was devastating. I felt my knees getting weak, and my heart seemed as if it was about to beat out of my chest.

The goon walked me over to the bed and forcefully pushed me down on it. "Beatrice!" I yelled as I crawled to her and hugged her tightly. Her lips were purple and her body was ice-cold.

She was long gone, and somewhere in the plan, we had failed, and this was the end result. I couldn't believe she was dead.

They watched me and laughed as I cried my eyes out in agony. Joell had seen enough, and pulled me off of her. He grabbed me by my neck and stood me up against the wall. I was on my tip toes as I felt his strong hand wrap around my neck.

"You think you can touch me?" Joell asked rhetorically. "You can't kill me, bitch! You came barking up the wrong tree. I sniffed y'all out from day one. Since the day Beatrice approached me, I have been watching all of you. This game isn't for rookies, and I am far from a rookie, Sunshine!" he said with passion as he squeezed my neck so hard I was unable to breathe. I stared into his bloodshot red eyes with no fear, even though inside I was terrified. I wouldn't give him the satisfaction of knowing that he had achieved such a feat.

"Oh, okay. I see you are a tough one, huh?" Joell said as he unleashed his grip on me, letting me fall to the floor, panting for air. I held my neck as I tried to catch my breath, and I felt someone pick me up and toss me on the bed.

"I'ma break you down. I'm going to show you not to fuck with me," Joell said with a sinister look in his eyes.

"Kill me and get it over with," I said as I breathed heavily and sat up on the bed.

"I'm not going to kill you. But you are going to wish you were dead when I am done with you.

Joell's goons grabbed me and pinned me down while ripping my clothes off, leaving me completely nude. I tried to stop them, but they were much more powerful than I was, and I couldn't fight them off. I saw one goon pull down his pants, exposing his rock hard tool. I saw about twelve inches of nightmare. He straddled me while the other men held me down, and forcefully penetrated me, causing me to arch my back in complete anguish. No man had ever been inside of me, and my virginity was now being stripped from me in the worst way. I could feel my pussy being ripped open. It was so painful and so degrading, causing me to let out screams that were muffled by a hand. He went in and out of me violently. I could feel myself splitting, and the pain shot through my entire body. He was much too large for my rather small opening. I cried and yelled, but it was to no avail, as no one could hear me through the soundproofed rooms, and Joell and his crew had no intentions of stopping.

Once he was finished, he squirted semen all over my upper torso and face. Just when I thought the chaos was over, he switched positions with another goon, and then he began to have his way with me. Joell just sat and watched in pleasure as he got his sweet revenge. Tears continued to run down my face, but the yelling stopped as I quit fighting back.

The rape lasted for an entire hour, as his four goons took turns on me, leaving me bloody and sore. It reminded me of the torture that my stepfather used to put Anisa through, and I wished that my big sister was there to save me from this pain. They violated both holes, and left me in agonizing pain, curled up on the bed.

Once they were finished, Joell put a gun to my head and whispered sternly, "Go tell whoever sent you that they shouldn't have sent a woman to do a man's job. If I ever see you or any of them other bitches, you're going to end up like this bitch," he said as he threw his head in the direction of Beatrice dead body. With that, he left me in the room alone and traumatized.

I weakly looked over at Beatrice and whispered, "Sorry B! I am so sorry!" as the tears flowed.

Things were never the same after Beatrice died. We all were shaken. It felt like everything was falling down around us. We didn't feel safe in the Yitty anymore, so we all packed our shit and relocated to Miami. We all had aspirations of leaving the foul game alone. With Beatrice gone, we had a piece of us missing. Getting out of New York was mandatory. We had to worry about Joell retaliating even more, and also we had to worry about the Russians. We took their money without completing the job, so we knew that we had created another enemy; an enemy that we couldn't stand up against. That botched hit taught us that we were not invincible, and at any time we could be gone. I hate that it took me being raped and Beatrice's death to teach us that hard lesson, but nevertheless, it was taken in heed. We moved with precision and intelligence from that day forward. We buried our girl in the Bronx, her hometown, and never looked back.

When we moved down to Miami, we tried our best to stay straight, but the allure of the game called for us, and when the money was low, we went back into business. We hooked up with a Haitian named Ma'tee, a powerful drug trafficker in Miami, and the rest is history. We never had any problems, except for the day we took on our biggest hit . . . The Cartel.

Chapter Fifteen

The Cartel

"Have chu heard from Miamor?" Aries asked as she handed Robyn a moving box to carry into their new apartment. They were in L.A., living the life, and after months of functioning out of hotels, they finally decided to move into their first West Coast spot. Their apartment overlooked Santa Monica Beach. They had made sure to get a three bedroom, just in case Miamor decided to join them one day.

"Nah, I haven't heard from her since we left. She's too wrapped up in that mu'fucka, Carter. I can't believe she chose him over us. That's been our rule since the very beginning; Fuck a nigga! Get your paper! I guess she forgot about all of that," Robyn stated with a shoulder shrug as they made their way inside.

Aries placed the box she held in her hands on the floor and sat down to go through its contents.

She frowned when she opened it to find it full of envelopes that were addressed to Miamor. "Me think chu made a mistake and took some of Miamor's stuff out of storage. This box is full of old letters to she," she stated.

"It's probably just old letters from Murder," Robyn said. "I probably grabbed them by mistake. She stayed writing that nigga back in the day. You would have thought *he* was her man instead of Anisa's."

Aries had never met Murder, but she had heard a lot about him. "Miamor used to talk about he all de time," she recalled.

Robyn nodded her head as she continued to unpack boxes and rearrange their place. "Uh-huh. Between me and you, I think they had a little thing for each other. It was like after that shit happened to her and Beatrice, she wasn't really worried about no dudes. I think that rape fucked her head up more than anything. Then, when she met that nigga, Carter, she was on some other shit; talking that love bullshit."

"Me don't trust de' nigga, Carter. Me think Miamor is in over she head," Aries stated. "She might need us."

Robyn waved her hand in dismissal. "I ain't worried about Miamor. She made her decision. Nobody forced her to stay back in Miami. She can take care of herself."

Aries opened up one of the letters and read the intimate words that Murder had written Miamor. It was obvious to her that Miamor and Murder had been close. In his letter, he expressed his concern for her, and also expressed how he wished he could take care of both Miamor and Anisa. It seemed like he was the only other male attachment Miamor had ever had.

Aries went into her room and pulled out a piece of paper. Robyn appeared in her doorway and asked, "What are you doing, girl? We still have so much stuff to unpack out of the car," she came in and flopped down on Aries' bed.

"Don't chu think it's strange that she hasn't even called us? We haven't gone one day without talking since de' day we met. Now all of a sudden, Mia just falls off the map. Me gut tells me something is wrong," Aries said.

"You're right," Robyn stated.

"Me think me's going to write Murder and let he know what's up with she," Aries said.

"What is he going to do? He's locked up," Robyn replied.

Aries showed Robyn the letter she had just read from Murder. "According to this, he will be out soon. Maybe he can talk some sense into she."

"A'ight, girl, go for what you know," Robyn

stated. She hugged Aries and left her to write her letter.

Murder walked on the platform of his tier, his khaki jail pants hanging slightly off of his behind as he strolled toward his cell. He received much love from the other inmates, but he didn't deal with many. His business was still popping in prison. He survived in the joint by murking niggas who stepped out of line. He was paid with cigarettes, drugs, shoes, clothes, books, and basically whatever else an inmate had to offer. It was far less than what he had killed for while he was on the outside, but behind the walls was a completely different world. Something as simple as a pack of cigarettes could be as worthy as gold in prison. He entered his cell just as the bars began to close.

A CO walked by. "Brown, you've got some mail," the fat white guard said as he stuck a single envelope through the bars of his cell.

A look of surprise crossed Murder's face. He only received mail from one person, but he hadn't heard from her in years. Miamor was the only person who had ever contacted him while he was locked up. He opened the letter and read:

Hey Murder:

Chu' don't know me, but I'm a friend of Miamor's. Me know chu know all about the Murder Mamas and what we are about. Anisa used to tell us stories about chu, so me know what chu about and how chu get down.

Anisa was killed down in Miami, and me think de' same people who killed she may have hurt Miamor too. She started fucking with one of our marks, and me thinks she is in trouble. Chu' are de only person who she might listen to. Please call me so that me can put her on three-way. Maybe chu can talk some sense into she. 852-444-9683. Me put some money on de' commissary for chu. Call soon.

Aries

Murder knew exactly who Aries and Robyn were. Miamor had told him all about them in some of her letters. He was now worried about Miamor. He didn't know what was going on, but he fully intended on finding out. He was up for parole, and would be out the joint in a couple of weeks. He wrote Aries back and asked her and Robyn to meet him in Miami. He had done five years easily, but now that he knew Miamor was in danger, the next two weeks were going to creep by torturously slow. *I know li'l mama better be a'ight, or niggas in Miami gon' bleed!*

Chapter Sixteen

The Cartel

Mecca stood over Miamor and looked at her with pure hatred. He had finally gotten a chance to be alone with her without any supervision, and he was going to make the most out of that opportunity. It was in between the nurse's shift, and his heart was racing as he looked down at his worst enemy. He wanted to tell Carter about Miamor, but he didn't want to take the chance of Carter siding with her. He saw how much Carter loved Miamor, and it enraged him, knowing that Carter loved the same woman that he hated so much. The last thing he wanted was to be in a beef with his only remaining blood brother over a female. He figured that what Carter didn't know, couldn't hurt him. *This bitch got his head gone, but I'm about to end this game and send her to her Maker,* he thought as he stared at her, clenching his jaws.

Mecca looked over his shoulder and made sure no one was coming just before he focused his attention back on his worst enemy. He bent down and began to whisper in Miamor's ear, hoping to God that she could hear him. He was unaware that she had come out of her coma earlier that day, so when she opened her eyes, it startled him. He saw the lazy look in her eyes and knew that she was weak. He was glad that she was conscious. Now she would know who was taking her life. Mecca was about to gain his sweet revenge.

"I hate you, bitch!" Mecca whispered as he began to pinch her oxygen supply. "I want you to die a slow death. I'ma finish what Fabian couldn't do," he whispered and he smirked as he heard her heart monitor begin to beep faster.

Miamor wanted to return the gesture by saying, "Fuck you!" but she was too weak to even open her mouth. The only thing she could move was her fingers.

Mecca looked down at her hand and noticed that she managed to stick her middle finger out. He chuckled as he pulled the pillow from under her head. Stopping her oxygen flow wasn't quick enough for him. He wanted her dead. He held the pillow up and prepared to suffocate her to death.

Miamor tried again to say something, tried to call for Carter, but only a low raspy grunt came out.

"Nobody can save you now, bitch!" Mecca whispered.

"What's going on?" Carter asked as he walked into the room.

"I was just fluffing her pillow, bro. Your sleeping beauty looked uncomfortable," Mecca said as he began to fluff the pillow, hoping that Carter didn't see what he was really trying to do.

Carter smiled and walked over to Mecca and put his hand on his shoulder. "I'll take it from here," he said, not knowing that Mecca was just about to murder his only true love. "I have to talk to you and Zyir when I finish up in here," Carter added, thinking about the plan that he was putting together for their relocation.

"Cool. I'll be downstairs," Mecca said just before he shot Miamor a cold stare.

Miamor matched his stare, and she wished that she could say something. Mecca and Miamor both despised each other with equal passion, and it was obvious that neither of them wanted to tell Carter the truth. Both of them wanted to kill one another and still keep a bond with an unknowing Carter.

Mecca exited, and Carter focused his attention on Miamor. He pulled up a chair to her bed and began to stroke her hair and look into her eyes. "Hey, beautiful," he said just before he leaned over and kissed her cheeks. He heard Miamor grunt while moving her lips, trying to talk.

"Shhh. Save your energy, baby," he said as he put his finger over her lips. "The nurse said it will take a couple of days before you will be able to talk or sit up. You just have to rest," he explained.

Miamor looked into Carter's brown eyes and knew that he was the man that she wanted to spend her life with. However, she knew that Mecca was trying to kill her. *I wish I could just tell him. Come on, Miamor, move your lips. Talk!* she thought as she tried to say something. But it was to no avail. I have to tell him the truth. Will he still love me? Will he understand and pick me over Mecca.

Carter picked up Miamor's hand and kissed it softly. "I am going to kill whoever did this to you, I swear. I know it's all my fault. I was in the middle of a war and never thought about my enemy coming for you," he said, feeling guiltier with every word.

Your brother is the one trying to kill me! Miamor thought as she heard the sincerity in his voice. She promised herself that if Mecca didn't kill her, she would tell Carter the truth as soon as she was able to. She was tired of running from herself. She was looking into the eyes of the future. Her future was in Carter Jones.

"Just listen," Carter said slowly and sternly. "After you get well, we are moving from Miami. No more wars no more of the fast life. We can work on us and become one," he said, meaning every word of what he was saying. He wanted to spend the rest of his life with Miamor, and he was willing to give up the dope game for good just to make that happen.

Carter couldn't take Miami's ills anymore. Breeze's death was the last straw. It was as if Breeze had died twice, because just when they were coming to terms that she was gone, she reappeared, but only to commit suicide when they were only seconds away from saving her. Carter was tired of everything . . . everything except for Miamor. *She is the only thing good in my life,* he thought as he clenched his jaw, thinking about his deep love for her. Just to see her lying in that bed helpless almost brought a tear to his eye. He was ready to make her a happy woman, and eventually, his wife.

A tear slipped down Miamor's cheek, and Carter believed it was tears of joy. But in actuality, it was a tear of pain. It pained Miamor to think about how she would have to tell him that she was connected to the man that killed most of his family, that she gave the drink to Taryn that killed her, and that she was a killer—a cold killer.

The nurse had just arrived, and Carter looked back, greeted her with a smile and stood up. "Get some rest. I will be back to check on you in a while," he said as he pecked her on the forehead and exited the room gracefully.

"Man, what the fuck is wrong with you?" Zyir asked half jokingly as he watched Mecca take a shot of Patrón.

Mecca was noticeably angry and irritated. "Nothing. I'm good, Zy," he said, thinking about how he couldn't get to Miamor. *I'ma kill that bitch tonight. I don't give a fuck. She's got to die,* he thought as he tried to conceal his feelings from Zyir, who was staring at him like he was crazy.

"You sweating and shit. I'm just saying, you look like you got something on your mind," Zyir said as he sat on the couch.

Before Mecca could respond, Carter entered the room. "Yo fam, I need to talk to y'all for a minute," Carter said as he sat on the Italian leather couch next to Zyir. Mecca sat across from them and wanted to hear what Carter had to say.

"Our time has passed with this organization. We have to clean our money and get out of the game. I have been talking to a couple of business associates, and I'm putting something together for us in Phoenix. We can wash our money and get into the casino business."

"A casino?" Zyir asked as he sat up, not expecting to hear what was coming out of Carter's mouth.

"That's right, Zy. We have to get out of the dope game and go legit. Some business partners of mine are willing to sell us a small share of a new casino that's being built there. It's the only way that we are going to ever prosper. The Feds are on me, and the connect ain't fucking with me because of the indictment. We are in a lose-lose situation. It's only a matter of time before The Cartel goes under, feel me?"

"What you talking about? Diamonds move dope! We run these streets, and I'm going to run these mu'fuckas until I die. Just like Poppa did," Mecca said, sounding more ignorant with every word.

"That's the mentality that's going to land us all in jail. Think about it, Mecca," Carter said as he emphasized his words with subtle hand gestures. "If snitch-ass Ace would not have had a baby mama, I would be serving a life sentence right now. We just barely got out of that situation, Mecca. We are under a microscope, and next time, I might not be so lucky!" Carter said, breaking down the truth to his younger brother.

"Maybe Carter is right," Zyir added as he began rubbing his hands together. "We have to get out of this 'hood mentality and expand. Think about not having to worry about, 'are we going to get caught' or 'whose next to die'. We're losing those we love behind this shit," he said as he thought of Breeze. "I'm with it," Zyir conceded as he held out his hand and slapped hands with Carter.

"Mecca, you in?" Carter asked as he and Zyir looked at him.

Yeah, I'm in, but first I got to kill your girl, Mecca thought as a small smirk appeared on his face. He was going to have fun killing Miamor. The fact that he was doing it right under Carter's nose added more enjoyment for him. "I'm in, bro," he said as he reached over and slapped Carter's hand.

"Good, good," Carter said as he stood up. "Look, but first we need to finish off the last shipment. We have to get our money out of the streets. Anybody that owes us money from consignment needs to pay up. We are out of the game officially today. I know that the business slowed down while I was locked up, but now I'm home, and it's time to collect. Zyir, I want you to collect from them Liberty City niggas, and Mecca, you need to collect from the Overtown crew. We hit them each with fifty joints, right?" Carter asked, not sure of the amounts that they had spotted the crew with on the previous shipment.

"Yeah, that's about right. I haven't heard from any of them either," Zyir added as he thought about the money that they had in the streets.

"Niggas thought that they wouldn't have to pay up since you got locked up. They think The Cartel is over. It's time for them niggas to pay," Mecca added as Carter refreshed his memory. "I almost forgot about that debt they owe us."

"I didn't," Carter added as he stood up to walk out of the room. "It's time for The Cartel to collect," he added just before he disappeared in the darkness of the hallway.

Zyir grabbed his keys, and so did Mecca. "I'm going to head out and take care of that," Zyir said, planning to head to Liberty City.

"Me too," Mecca said as his trigger finger began to itch.

He wanted to go and put a bullet in Miamor's head so badly, but he decided to wait until he came back. He wanted Miamor to be in fear. She didn't need to know when he would kill her, but she knew he was lurking, and that was enough to plant his seed of fear. He wanted to make her miserable before taking her life. Mecca smiled and headed out of the door, followed closely by Zyir.

Miamor watched as the nurse dipped the towel in the soapy wash pan. It pained Miamor to know that she was helpless and couldn't move on her own. *I feel so weak*, she thought as she felt the warm towel on her skin. Mecca constantly stayed on her mind. She didn't know when he would return to kill her, and she knew that he would succeed, because she was too weak to defend herself. She saw a man's silhouette in the door and her heart began to speed up, hoping that it wasn't Mecca.

Before she could play the guessing game, Carter appeared, leaning in the doorway. "How is she doing?" he asked as he slowly walked in.

"She is going to be fine. She just needs a lot of rest and love," the nurse said as she continued to wipe Miamor's arms and neck, cleaning her.

"Great," Carter said as he leaned over and kissed Miamor's forehead. He stared at Miamor, and couldn't wait until he took her away from the chaos. He had already decided that he would ask her to marry him and be his forever. But first, he would have to nurse her back to health.

***

"Yeah, that's the nigga right there," Robyn said as she watched Mecca and Zyir leave the house. "The Dominican on the right, that's Mecca Diamond, and the other one is Carter's li'l nigga, Zyir." Murder clenched his jaw and breathed heavily through his nose as they camped in a truck outside of the Diamond's estate. They had been eyeing the place for hours, because Murder wanted to check out what he was going up against. He wanted to find Miamor, but first, he would have to find Carter.

"He's the one that killed Anisa?" he asked as he grinded his teeth together, feeling the anger building up inside of himself.

"Yeah, that's him," Aries added as she remembered when Anisa was murdered.

Murder didn't get the name "Murder" for nothing, and he was good at what he did. That's why he always checked out the competition before just jumping into the situation blindly. He knew he would kill Mecca in due time, but he would have to be patient. His main concern was finding Miamor.

Zyir and Mecca got into two different cars, and they pulled out. Murder decided to follow Zyir, hoping he would lead him to Carter or Miamor.

***

Zyir slowly nodded his head to Nas as he maneuvered his car through the streets of Liberty City. He smiled as thoughts of Breeze invaded his mind, and just as quickly as the thought lit up his world, it brought him down. He blinked away tears as he thought about how their relationship never got the chance to grow. She had been taken away from him before they could build their love, and he missed her in a new way as each day passed. He looked at the picture he had of her on his dashboard, and gripped the steering wheel tightly as visions of her hanging crossed his mind. He checked his rearview, and noticed a white truck that had been behind him for a minute. *What the fuck?* He thought to himself as he switched lanes, and just as he expected, the truck switched lanes also. He then knew he was being followed. Just to be sure, he made two rights hitting each block with speed, and the truck followed him. Zyir reached under his seat and pulled out his Tech-nine. He set it on his lap and glanced at the truck once again. He wasn't about to play the "cat and mouse" game, so he decided to see what was happening. He approached a red light, and the white truck was behind him about two car lengths. He tried to look and see who the driver was, but the black tint kept him or her a mystery.

Zyir threw his gear into park and hopped out with his gun in hand. He pointed at the truck as he walked toward it. "What's good, my nigga?" he yelled as his jaw tightened and he was ready for whatever. He couldn't see who was behind the glass, so he hesitated to squeeze. The truck burned rubber and sped past him, as Zyir kept his gun on the vehicle. He pointed the Tech at the truck until it was out of sight. He didn't know who was following him, but they were about to get aired out by his little friend.

Zyir hopped back in his car and headed to Liberty City to pick up the rest of The Cartel's money. "Whew!" he huffed as he turned up the music and proceeded. "Maybe, I'm tripping," he said, pulling off.

Chapter Seventeen

The Cartel

Six Weeks Later

Carter's eyes were bloodshot red as he sat near Miamor's bedside. His worry for her had taken a toll on his body. He hadn't gotten a good night's sleep since finding her, because he sat in the rocking chair in her room all day and night to make sure that she was okay. He was grateful that she had come out of her coma, but she was still so weak, and he felt that he needed to be strong for her. He wanted to keep her spirits up until she was fully recovered. He leaned forward in his chair and rested his elbows on his knees as he sighed. He watched her stir in her sleep slightly.

"No . . . no . . . !" she groaned while still asleep. She began to struggle and lash out as if she were fighting someone.

Carter stood and approached her bedside. "Miamor," he said. "Wake up, ma."

"No!" she screamed as she sat straight up in bed and fought against Carter. It was dark in the room, and Miamor had been dreaming of Mecca killing her. When she awoke and found a man by her bed, she thought that he had come for her again. She was sweating and her breathing was labored. She was shaking, the terror in her heart paralyzing her while her eyes darted wildly around the room.

"Miamor, it's me, baby . . . it's just me!" Carter said soothingly as he held on to her tightly.

When Miamor heard Carter's voice she broke down in his arms. "He's going to kill me!" she sobbed as she held on to him like a frightened little girl clinging to her father.

Concern was written all over Carter's face. He grabbed her by the shoulders and forced her to look into his eyes. "Who, Miamor? You have to tell me who you're afraid of," Carter said. He was determined that when he found out the identity of Miamor's attacker, he was going to kill him.

Miamor saw the sincerity in his eyes, which only made her cry harder.

He sighed and pulled her to his chest. "Shh. It's okay, ma. I'm not going to let anything happen to you. I almost lost you once. I won't lose you again," he promised.

He scooped Miamor into his arms and carried her to the rocking chair. He sat down with her and stroked her hair while he rocked back and forth.

"I can't stay here, Carter," she whispered. She gripped the collar of shirt in fear. She was holding on to him for dear life.

"Shh . . . I got you, ma. I promise you—"

"Carter, no!" Miamor yelled as she sat up shakily and looked at him with sad eyes. She wanted to be a part of this charade. She wanted to live here with him, but with Mecca around, her life would always be at risk. "I can't live in this house. I don't feel safe here. I won't stay here, Carter. If you try to make me, I'll run. I'm like a sitting fucking duck in this bitch!" she cried. She had never been this emotional, but since coming out of her coma, her fear had rendered her helpless and feeble. All she did lately was cry. "He can touch me here. I have to go to a place where he can't find me."

"*Who*, Miamor? Who the fuck is after you? I can't help you if you don't talk to me," Carter said in frustration. "I'll handle that nigga. You don't have to run. You don't have to worry about it if you just trust me. Give me your burdens, ma," he whispered as he put his hand gently behind her head and pressed his forehead against hers.

Miamor desperately wanted to give her all to him. She wanted to put her life in his hands, but how could she, when the one man she feared on this earth was Carter's flesh and blood? She hated Mecca just as much as she loved Carter. *If I show him who I really am, I'm going to lose him,* she thought as she shook her head and kissed his lips. "I can't Carter. You would never understand. Just please get me out of here. Right now. I need to feel safe," Miamor pleaded.

It hurt Carter that after all they had been through, Miamor still didn't trust him enough to feel secure in his home. He tried to understand where she was coming from. He figured that she was just paranoid from her attack. She was afraid, and he was determined to give her a sense of security. "All right, ma. Let me get you dressed then we'll go. We'll go wherever you want to go," he assured her. He placed her back in the bed and put a pair of sweat pants on her.

He touched her with such gentleness that it made Miamor yearn for him, not in a sexual way, but in an emotional way. He was so stable. He was always so focused and in control. Every move that he made was calculated concisely. Miamor wanted to depend on him and take his lead, but it could never happen. In the grand scheme of things, they would always be adversaries. Like Romeo and Juliet, their allegiances lay on different sides, while their hearts were in each other's hands.

"Let me get your pain medication. It's in the master bedroom. I'll be right back," Carter said before kissing the top of her head.

She nodded and watched him disappear into the hallway. *This man is my soul mate, but we can never be together,* she thought grimly.

She looked over to the nightstand that was beside the rocking chair. A gun lay on top of it. She swung her legs over the edge of the bed, wincing in pain as she stood to her feet. Her legs felt like Jell-O, but she used all her energy to make it over to the stand. She leaned against it and took deep breaths as she grabbed the gun. Holding the pistol in her hand caused a wave of relief to wash over her. She gripped it as her head hung on her chest, and she inhaled deeply.

Miamor had been through hell, and she would never be the same woman that she was before. Her body was scarred for life. She would never be able to forget what had happened, because the war wounds would be a constant reminder of her plight. Like a Jew who had been terrorized by Hitler or a slave that had been victimized by their master, Miamor would always remember. She would always feel the pain; she would always harbor fear, resentment, and insecurity . . . she would never forget. Mecca had changed her life for the worst, and now she had to refocus. She had to retrain her body, and she had to regain composure over her emotions, because she was determined to get back at Mecca. But, she didn't have a choice but to wait. She had to give herself time to heal.

Carter came back into the room and frowned when he saw Miamor standing. He rushed over to her. "What are you doing? You shouldn't be on your feet," he said. His eyes went to the gun in her hands. He tried to take it from her, but she shook her head.

"Don't, Carter. I need it," she whispered seriously.

Carter picked her up, and with the gun in her hand he carried her out of the room.

All of the luxury inside of the house meant nothing to Miamor. By being there, she was in Mecca's territory, and she refused to stay. She clung to her man and kept her finger on the trigger of the gun as he carried her outside to his car. After making sure that she was secure in the passenger seat, he hurried around to the driver's side, and they pulled away.

***

Murder sat up in his seat when he saw Carter carrying Miamor out of his house. It was the first time he had seen her in five long years, and it was evident that she was badly injured. His blood boiled at the thought of someone putting their hands on her, and the intimate way that Carter handled her enraged Murder even more. *I'ma handle that nigga personally,* he thought as he palmed his pistol and leaned low in his seat as he watched Carter drive by. Murder pulled out into traffic and followed. This was the opportunity he had been waiting patiently for. There were no bodyguards surrounding Carter. *It's just me and him. This mu'fucka riding around with my shorty like she's his bitch,* Murder thought angrily. *I'ma bout to claim that, and wipe him and his people off the map.*

Murder made sure that he kept Carter's car in sight. Now that he had seen Miamor, he was more determined than ever to bring her home.

Anger pulsed through Carter as he drove in silence. He was livid, not with Miamor, but with whoever had instilled so much fear in her heart. He stroked her hand reassuringly as he sped through the city streets, headed toward the Four Seasons Hotel. Miamor didn't ask him where he was taking her. She trusted that he would take her to a place where she couldn't be touched.

When they arrived, Carter didn't let Miamor's feet touch the ground. Seeing her so broken was tearing him up inside. All he wanted to do was treat her like his queen, and if tucking her away inside a fortress was what she wanted, then he would give it to her. He picked her up, and she nestled her head into his chest. He tucked the gun inside of his jacket so that it wouldn't be visible as he took her inside.

"I need your Presidential Suite," Carter said to the front desk clerk. The young man behind the desk looked awkwardly at Carter, who was still holding his woman in his arms. "Now!" Carter reinforced with authority.

When Carter entered the room, he lay Miamor down on the bed. "Close your eyes, ma. You're safe here. Nobody knows where you are but me," he said as he pulled the duvet up to cover her battered body.

Tears accumulated in her eyes until they were so full that they had nowhere else to go but down her face. "Will you hold me?" she asked.

Carter removed his clothes as Miamor's eyes took him in. Her love button began to throb as she admired his chiseled abdomen and chest. He stood before her in nothing, but his boxers.

He was exquisite . . . the ideal specimen of a man in every way. He was the Adam to her Eve, but seeing his perfection brought about her insecurity as she reached up to touch her face. She had yet to look at herself in a mirror, but she knew that she didn't look the same. Her face felt differently, as if Mecca's fists and torturous beating had rearranged her features in the worst possible composition.

Carter climbed into the bed and spooned Miamor from the back.

"I can't keep you," she whispered. "I'm all fucked up. I can feel it. My face isn't the same. Everything about me is fucked up. My body, my face, my heart, my soul." She spoke so low that Carter could barely hear her.

"You can't keep me away from you, ma," Carter said, his lips gracing her ear. He stood up and retrieved a mirror from the vanity. He brought it over to Miamor.

Her hands shook as she reached for the antique handle. When her face came into view, she had to put her hand over her mouth to stop herself from crying too loudly. She could not bear to look at herself. Her face was almost unrecognizable. The left side of her face suffered a broken jaw, and was healing, but remained swollen and bruised. The blood vessels near her left eye were permanently damaged, and a green bruise would always remain near her temple, not to mention the many cuts that marred her once smooth skin. Everything that she loved about herself was non-existent. All of her perfect features were destroyed. "How can you even stand to look at me?" she asked as she tossed the mirror aside. "I'm not even the same woman you used to know." Now, her face reflected the way she had always felt inside . . . ugly, scarred, and bruised. She had always felt like damaged goods.

"Miamor, you're beautiful, ma. Everything about you is beautiful," Carter whispered as he climbed back in bed with her, holding her tight. "Do you know how fucked up I was when I thought I'd never see you again?" Miamor didn't answer, so he continued. "I was lost, ma. You were made for me. These scars show you're a fighter. You're supposed to be dead right now, but you're not. Your body will heal, Miamor. You just have to give it time. But I love you for what's inside you. You're my lady, forever," he whispered as he took her hand and held it up for her to see. He knew that she had been in so much pain lately that she never even realized that he had slipped a diamond ring onto her finger. She gasped when she finally noticed it. "Be my wife."

Miamor was sobbing so hard that she could not form the words to respond. Carter kissed the back of her neck. "I don't want to see you cry, ma," he whispered. "I know you love me, Miamor, but you refuse to let me all the way in. Trust me. Let me protect you. Let me see all of you."

"You won't like what you see," Miamor admitted with sorrow in her tone.

Carter's lips made their way south as he kissed from the back of her neck to her shoulders, to her back, and further on. He parted her legs and slipped his tongue between her thighs.

The intense pleasure temporarily erased her pain as a sigh escaped from her lips. "You don't really know me," Miamor moaned as she allowed him to kiss her inner thigh. She could see the top of his head as he slowly traced the creases of her vagina with his tongue.

"Teach me," he responded. He pulled her southern lips apart, revealing her pearl. "Trust me," he said as he took it into his mouth, causing Miamor to squirm underneath him. "Marry me," he whispered as his tongue made love to her clit, plucking it like a delicate flower.

The heat from his mouth drove her crazy, and her eyelids closed in ecstasy. Her love for this man was so deep, that from the very first time she saw him, she knew he was her Achilles heel. He was one of the few people who had actually ever gotten her to feel. She experienced emotions with him that she never knew existed. He had found her and nursed her back to health. He loved her despite her appearance, but she was not sure that he would accept her once he found out who she really was. Her soul rained as teardrops graced her cheeks. Her cry was inaudible, but her heart was bleeding for the love that she needed, but she knew that it was one she could never have.

Carter worked her over until she came in his mouth. Her love came down like a waterfall, and Carter licked her clean, sucking her clit until her legs shook in satisfaction. He arose silently and walked into the bathroom and drew her a bath.

The feelings he had for Miamor made him weak, but it was a weakness that he embraced. She made him a better man, and no matter what she said, she would always belong to him. He wasn't taking "no" for an answer. He was so torn up about what had happened to her. He blamed himself every day. He just wanted to make her happy. After everything he had lost in the war with the Haitians, she was all he had left. As he sat on the side of the tub and watched it fill with water, he felt himself becoming emotional. *I let this happen to her,* he thought.

He felt her arms envelop him, and he looked up to see her standing there. Her health had come a long way since the day he had found her close to dead in the hospital, but she still needed to rest. He knew that it had taken a lot out of her to come and check on him. As he looked up into her eyes, he saw the woman his heart was meant for. She was a fighter, but he didn't want her to have to endure anymore anguish. He had to be strong for her. He quickly restored his composure and pulled her down onto his lap.

"I'm sorry I wasn't there to protect you," he whispered, his words stopping in his throat.

Hearing the stress in his voice caused Miamor to close her eyes in torment. *I have to tell him. I can't let him think that he did this to me. I can't hurt him like this. He thinks he loves me, but he doesn't even know the real me. I'm the reason why everyone he loves is dead. I can't marry him. There is no way that we can ever be together,* she thought dismally. Even if she agreed to marry Carter, in her heart of hearts, she knew that it would never happen. Their wedding would turn into somebody's funeral, because he was sure to find out about her affiliation with the Murder Mamas and her role in Taryn and Breeze's misfortunes. She also did not trust herself, because as soon as she crossed Mecca's path, she knew that she would get it popping.

I am not the housewife type. If you really love him, then you will let him go, she told herself over and over. Miamor had to convince herself that their love affair was over just to stop herself from yearning for his touch. Carter was like a drug to her. She had become addicted to his swagger; the way he walked; the way he talked; the unspoken boss status that he possessed' the way he smiled . . . all of it endeared her to him. She was willing to settle down, willing to be faithful, willing to trust him. She was ready, but she had to walk away. Out of everything she had been through, leaving Carter would undoubtedly be the hardest thing she ever had to do. *I don't have a choice,* she told herself. She hoped that Carter would remember them for what they were to each other before all of the shit had been thrown into the game. He would always hold a special place in her heart. Miamor wiped away a tear as she closed her eyes.

"Carter, I have to tell you something," she uttered as she massaged the back of his head gently. Knowing that it would be the last time she would ever touch him, she took her time and stared him in his eyes. "I'm not who you—"

Before Miamor could get the words out of her mouth, Carter's lips covered hers. He kissed her passionately as he removed the hotel robe she was wearing. He didn't want to make love to her. She was still too weak for that. He just wanted to take care of his queen, to nurture his woman, to sit back and spend time with his future wife. He removed his Calvin Klein boxers and pulled her gently into the tub.

"Carter, I really need to tell you this—"

"Shh!" his lips never left hers as he silenced her. "If you're not saying "yes", then I don't want to hear it. Will you marry me?" he asked.

A lump formed in Miamor's throat. How could she tell him no? She nodded her head and gave him a weak smile. "Yes," she answered, but as soon the words left her mouth, she knew that she had made a mistake. *In the morning . . . I'll tell him tomorrow,* she told herself.

The next morning, Carter awoke to find Miamor staring at him. Her eyes were swollen and red from crying all night as she watched him sleep.

"What's wrong, ma? Everything a'ight?" he asked as the palm of his hand graced her face. "Are you in pain?"

"More than you can even understand," she admitted.

"I'ma take all of that away, Mia," he said. "We're moving to Phoenix. I've already begun making the arrangements. In a week, we'll be miles away from Miami."

Miamor put her finger to his lips. "Carter, I need to tell you something. There is something that I need to get off my chest. It's important."

Carter frowned. He could see the worried look in her eyes. There was something heavy on her mind, and he wanted her to know that she could tell him anything. "Just say it, Miamor. You can talk to me."

"First, I want you to know that everything I feel for you is real. It's more real than anything I've ever known. I love you more than I've ever loved anyone in the world. You mean everything to me, Carter, but I can't accept this ring," she said as she removed it from her finger.

"Don't do this, Miamor," he said. "Don't shut me out."

Miamor stood up and paced the room, her wobbly legs barely able to keep her up. *Just tell him,* she urged herself. "Carter, there's a lot about me that you don't know. I've been lying to you—never about how I feel—but all along, you never knew who I really was. Ma'tee paid me and my girls to get at The Cartel!"

Carter sat up in the bed and his eyes instantly turned cold. He stood and put his hands on the wall as he lowered his head and absorbed her words.

"I belong to a group called the Murder Mamas. We've hit niggas from New York to the South. Ma'tee paid us to come at Mecca, but he ended up killing my sister, Anisa. I've been at him ever since, but he got to me first. He beat the shit out of me. All these cuts and bruises came from him, all because he knew who I was. He gave me a poisoned drink at your sister's memorial, but I gave it to Taryn. I knew the drink Mecca had given me had something in it, and I gave it to her anyway. I was willing to do anything to get back at Mecca for taking my sister away. When I first met you, I didn't know you were a part of The Cartel!" Miamor cried.

Carter was calm, as he used the wall for support. He was too calm for what she was telling him, and she had a bad feeling in the pit of her stomach, but she still continued her confession.

"Carter, you have to believe me. If I had known that you were a part of it, I would have never fucked with you. I came to your brother's funeral to kill Mecca. That's when I found out who you were, but by then, it was too late. I had already fallen for you. I love you Carter, but there is something wrong with me inside. Killing is all I know. I've been doing it since I was twelve years old. You don't know me! I'm a bitch! I'm a Murder Mama! I'm heartless and cold! I'm all of these things, except when I'm with you. You are the only person in my entire life who has ever taken my pain away!"

Carter clenched his teeth as he listened to Miamor's story. The realization of who she really was hit him like a ton of bricks. The thousand lies that she had told him were a slap in the face. It was all too much for him to even comprehend. He could feel his anger rising as he thought of how he had trusted her. He had made the mistake of letting her get close. All this time, he had been sleeping with the enemy. She had been plotting on him while he had been investing his time and commitment into her. She had played him. He thought of the day he had seen her at Monroe's funeral, and then the faces of his deceased loved ones popped into his mind. She had contributed to the madness, and he had allowed her to. Everything had gone down right underneath his nose. Mecca had tried to warn him about her treachery, but Carter had refused to see. *That's why he hates her so much!* he thought.

Miamor walked over to Young Carter. His silence was killing her. "Please, say something!" she begged.

Carter didn't even feel himself react until it was too late.

Smack!

His rage took over, and he slapped her with such force that it sent her flying to the ground. She instantly tasted the salty blood that oozed from her busted lip.

Carter stormed over to the nightstand where he had stored his gun. Miamor's eyes grew large when she saw him approach her with it in his hands. He loaded the clip and cocked it back, then knelt down over her. With tears in his eyes, he grabbed her hand forcefully. "Take the gun, bitch!" he mumbled through clenched teeth as he held the barrel up to his chest while she gripped the handle. "You wanted to get back at The Cartel that bad? Do you know how many innocent people you've hurt? Pull the trigger, Miamor. I *am* The Cartel! Now is your chance!"

Miamor lay beneath Carter with the gun in her shaky hands. "Carter, don't do this!" she beseeched.

"Kill me, you grimy bitch! This is what you wanted. I told you I'd give you anything. You wanted this, so I'm giving it to you." Carter was so livid that he was foaming at the mouth, and his grip was so tight on her hand that it felt like her bones would crush from the pressure.

Miamor had never let anybody test her or even speak to her in such a way. Carter was pulling her card, and her murderous instincts clicked back in slightly as she glared into his eyes. He was challenging her, calling her bluff, daring her to shoot him. *This mu'fucka must not know,* she thought as her nostrils flared. Miamor was like a pit bull. When she was docile, she was one of the most loyal and gentle creatures in the world. But when provoked, something inside of her snapped, and once she clicked on, it was very hard to turn her off.

Miamor's finger wrapped around the trigger, but when she looked into the eyes of the man she loved, she could not bring herself to finish what she had started. Too many things had changed. Her heart wasn't as cold as it used to be. "I can't!" she wept. "I can't!"

Carter snatched the gun from her and put it to her head, pressing it point blank range as his finger danced on the hair trigger. Hatred and betrayal was in the air as he contemplated ending her life. She had peeled away at his outer layers, the same way that he had done to her. They had penetrated each other's souls, which is why her treachery stung so much. He knew that he should kill her. She deserved to die, but not at his hands. He threw the gun across the room as he arose to his feet. "Get the fuck out," he said calmly, but Miamor didn't move. Instead, she rolled onto her side as she cried. She was paralyzed in her grief.

"I'm sorry!" she screamed.

"Bitch, get out!" Carter repeated. His voice roared throughout the suite, and he showed no mercy as he dragged Miamor across the hotel room floor, disregarding her already injured body.

"Carter, no! Please!" she yelled as she fought him. She was fighting to stay in his life. With all of the energy she had left, she was clinging to him because she knew that once she let go he would no longer be hers.

By the time he got her out of the suite, he was sweating and out of breath and she was curled up in the hallway. "What am I going to do?" she cried while looking up into his face.

He showed no emotion, no sympathy, no love as he turned on his heels and re-entered the room. He snatched her phone up then tossed it into the hallway beside her. "I don't give a fuck what you do, Miamor," he said, the tone of his voice revealing his disappointment. "I'm done.

You have got five minutes to call a cab. If you're not gone by then, I'm going to finish this, and unlike you, I *will* be able to pull the trigger," he threatened. He took one last look at her and shook his head in disgust.

She could see the hatred in his eyes. There was nothing left to say. It was over, and he had tossed her out with nothing. He slammed the door in her face, closing the best chapter of her life.

Chapter Eighteen

The Cartel

Miamor had never felt so low as she sat in the hallway of the luxury hotel, pleading with Carter to forgive her. Her ego and principles were thrown out of the window. When it came to matters of the heart, she was willing to look foolish and willing to swallow her pride if it meant that Carter would be with her. She cried her heart out to him through the closed door, but it never opened. He had shut her out of his life, and she had to accept it. She was physically and emotionally spent as she stood to her feet. Using the wall to hold her up, she made her way to the elevator. Her hair was wild, her face stained with dried tears, and she wore nothing but a bathrobe as she made her way out of the hotel. Stares and whispers surrounded her as her bare feet carried her through the lobby.

"Excuse me, Miss," the maître d'hôtel of the establishment rushed over to her with two security guards in tow. "I received a call from the Presidential Suite. I'm going to have to escort you off of the premises."

The security guards grabbed her arms and she snatched them away. "Don't touch me!" she screamed, making an even bigger scene. She made it outside and walked as far as her feet would take her, but every step felt like a thousand. She was too fragile to make it on her own. She had exhausted all of her energy, and gave up as she fell to the ground to catch her breath, the hot pavement burning her skin. At this point, she felt hopeless. She had given up everything and had betrayed her girls trying to chase a dream. At least before she had them as her family. Now, all she had was herself.

Murder had sat in the car all night watching the hotel, waiting to see Miamor and Carter emerge. He was so close to her, and he wasn't going anywhere until he brought her home, back to New York where she belonged. He cringed at the way Carter touched Miamor, and jealousy loomed over him like a dark cloud.

When he finally saw Miamor emerge from the hotel alone, struggling, and barefoot, he grabbed his gun and jumped out of the car and ran toward her. His baggy khaki shorts, white T-shirt and red fitted cap represented the complete opposite of what Carter's poised demeanor did, but the two men had one thing in common. They both loved Miamor.

"Miamor!" he yelled, grabbing her attention.

Miamor didn't even look in his direction. She heard a man screaming her name and instantly thought of Mecca. She looked around for something to defend herself with, but she could barely scrape herself off of the ground. She frantically tried to hide, but there was nowhere to go. Traumatized and too tired to put up a fight, she screamed when Murder finally reached her. It wasn't until he picked her up off the ground did she realize that she wasn't in danger.

"It's okay, ma. Murder's back. I'm gonna handle that nigga and anybody associated with him," he sneered. "Word to my mutha', ma. I'ma cook that beef personally!

Miamor thought that her eyes were deceiving her. "Murder?" she called out as she touched his face.

"It's me, shorty. I got you."

Relief washed over Miamor and she gave into her body's urge to rest. She closed her eyes, knowing that she was in the arms of family, and that nothing would happen to her while he was around. It had been five long years since she had felt that safe. It seemed like a lifetime ago since she had felt the secure connection with Murder. But now that she had seen his face again, she realized he was still so prevalent in her life. Even with Carter, there was the constant threat of danger, but with Murder, there were no secrets. No lies dwelled between them. There was only trust.

Murder took Miamor back to the motel room where Robyn and Aries were waiting. It was a far cry from the Four Seasons, but it was how he got down. Murder was not into the glamorous life. He wasn't a flashy type a nigga. He was a 'hood nigga and a goon who had established his track record in the 'hood from the sandbox up. He didn't need all the extras. He actually found the entire Cartel establishment to be a joke. *Those clown-ass niggas on that Hollywood Godfather shit,* he thought as he put Miamor down and stared at her. *That Rico Suave-ass nigga don't know how to keep a bitch like Miamor. Shorty a gangsta, not some high society broad.*

"What happened to she?" Aries asked as she and Robyn rushed to Miamor's side and observed their dear friend.

"That bitch-ass nigga, Mecca happened to her," Robyn stated as she shook her head and wiped away a tear. She and Miamor hadn't always seen eye to eye. They butted heads more than a little bit, but that's what family does. Miamor was her sister. They had been through the fire together, and to see her so beat up enraged her.

"That nigga, Carter let the shit happen to her. Mecca's his brother. He wanted to be her man, so he should have been her man and made sure she wasn't touched, nah mean?" Murder said. "He gonna feel it too."

Miamor heard the voices around her and slowly opened her eyes.

"How are you feeling, mama?" Robyn asked.

Miamor smiled slightly and shook her head from side to side. "I lost him!" she whispered.

Aries and Robyn looked at one another, and then back down to Miamor. They couldn't understand her love for Young Carter, and they were past the point of trying. They were just glad that they had gotten their friend out while she was still alive. They knew that Miamor no longer had the malice it took to kill, so they would handle it for her.

She doesn't even have to know, Robyn thought. *Once Carter and Mecca are out of the picture, she will be able to move on with her life. She'll be back to her old self in no time.*

"Chu have us, Mia," Aries stated. "That's all chu need."

"I'm so sorry for turning my back on y'all. You guys are all I have," Miamor said.

Robyn knew that Miamor wasn't herself, because she had never apologized for anything. The new, emotional woman in front of her was not the same girl she had met years ago. She wasn't the same chick who had cut off a nigga's dick for money, or the same one who had taught her to shoot a gun properly. Miamor had changed. She was vulnerable. *Love has really made her ass go soft,* Robyn thought.

"It's okay, honey. We're sisters. We're always here for you. Me and Aries are going to let you get some rest, but there's somebody else here for you," Robyn said as she stood. She grabbed Aries' hand and they exited the room.

Miamor turned her head and smiled when she saw Murder posted by the door, with one foot resting against the wall. He scanned her from head to toe. Neither of them said a word, but they stared intently at each other. They were both surveying the changes they saw in one another.

He finally walked over to Miamor and knelt beside the bed. He grabbed her hand and turned it over to see the tattoo on her wrist. "You still my li'l mama, huh?" he asked as he kissed the tattoo. He knew what the phrase "Murder Mama" meant. It meant that she was his, and she knew it too.

"Always," she replied as she touched his face, remembering the bond that they had once shared.

"I missed you, Miamor. I thought about you every day while I was on the island," he said.

She wiped a lone tear away and gave him a half smile. She used to think about Murder all the time, before she met Carter. "I missed you too," she responded.

Murder looked at her, and the anger inside of him was evident. It radiated off of him, and because she knew him so well, she was able to read him like a book. His presence was exactly as she remembered it. He was still strong and commanding as he had always been. Prison had done him good. He was solid and strong, his swagger still the same . . . low key and mysterious.

"I didn't want this for you, Miamor. This wasn't supposed to be your life," Murder stated as he kissed her hand.

"This is all I've ever known. Every time I find someone that I love, I realize that fate is playing a sick game with me. I can never have someone to call my own. You belonged to Anisa. Carter belongs to The Cartel. I wanted you both, but neither of you were meant for me," she said miserably, the sorrow of her broken heart affecting her words.

"I came to take you home," Murder stated.

"Ha!" Miamor laughed obnoxiously as she shook her head. "Home? I don't think I've ever had one of those. I've never been in one place long enough to consider it home. I've never felt safe enough to be 'at home'," she said. "Where's home for me, Murder?"

"With me," he stated simply.

Miamor knew that because Anisa wasn't around, things could be different between them. He loved her. He always had, but she wasn't an eighteen-year-old girl anymore. She was a grown-ass woman who had evolved. With her emotions for Carter all over the place, she didn't know how she felt. When she had come to Miami, she had put Murder out of her mind, but it was obvious to her that he had never forgotten about her. He had come for her after five long years, just as he had promised he would. He never broke his word to her. He would give her the world if he could. *Can I offer him the same loyalty in return?* she asked herself.

"I don't know if I can give you what you want from me right now, Murder. I've never lied to you, so I do not want to start now. My heart is with someone else," she admitted sadly. It was something that she did not want to say, but something that he had to hear.

Murder winced and released her hand. He hated Carter for locking down Miamor's heart. The look in her eye when she spoke of Carter was the same look that used to be reserved for him years ago. "That nigga almost cost you your life, Mia," he reminded.

"He didn't know what I was into . . ."

Murder heard her as she tried to defend him, but he interrupted. "Aw, ma, don't give me that. The nigga knew what *he* was into! That's all that matters. If he's a boss, then he protects those around him, especially his bitch. You know the game, ma. I know you know, cuz I taught you. You should have murked him, Miamor. Quick, and without a second thought, because that was the job you were paid to do. That was what you signed up for when you picked up that phone years ago. You're my li'l mama. You're Murder's mama baby, girl. You know what it is between me and you. That's why you got my name tatted on you."

Miamor turned up her lips and rolled her eyes as she sneered at him in denial. "We all got the same tattoo," she defended.

"Yeah, but it was your idea, and it meant the most to you," he said, knowingly. He smiled and lifted her chin, forcing her to reveal the truth in a smile of her own. After all this time, he still knew her all too well. "Forget about him, Miamor. I'm back now. I cared for your sister, but she's gone. Everything that stopped us before does not matter now. Nothing is in the way now. I came here for you, and another nigga will never hurt you while I'm around. Get some rest. We are leaving for New York in a couple days."

Chapter Nineteen

The Cartel

"We got to dead these niggas," Murder whispered as he looked over his shoulder to make sure Miamor was still asleep. He, Robyn and Aries were huddled up, putting their game plan in motion. Murder wanted what was left of The Cartel dead. He planned on killing Carter first, and then making Mecca come to them. He was about to set a trap for The Cartel.

Miamor was dead to the world, as she lightly snored in the bed just a couple of feet away from them. The painkillers that she had been taking had her drowsy, and for the past two days she had done nothing but sleep. She was still recovering from a coma, and also from a broken heart. It pained Murder to see her heartbroken over another man. He felt like Carter had stolen what was his. The Miamor he remembered was feisty and was never pressed over a dude. *This*

Carter guy really has her heart, Murder thought as a small streak of resentment ran through his body. He glanced over at Miamor and admired her beauty. Even with the marks and scars on her face, she was beautiful to him. He focused back on Aries and Robyn and spoke.

"We got to handle this dude," Murder said as his trigger finger began to itch.

"I know, but I cannot get to the nigga. Miamor is not going to help us murk him. She's in love with him," Robyn said, trying to explain to Murder how Miamor had changed.

"It's okay. We are going to make him come to us," Murder said as he put his plan together in his mind. He felt obligated to kill Mecca and Carter because of all the pain they had caused the only women who he had ever let into his life, Anisa and Miamor. He took the trespass against them personally, and he wasn't leaving Miami until all scores were settled.

"Grab Miamor's phone," he instructed Aries, as he had it all mapped out. Carter was about to die, and then Mecca soon after. He planned on using Miamor as bait.

Robyn walked over to the night stand and sneakily removed Miamor's cell phone. She walked back over to Murder and handed the phone to him. Murder quickly went into Miamor's contact list and began to scroll down, looking for Carter's name. He located it and quickly began to text him in hopes that Carter would think Miamor was texting him.

"I'ma make this nigga come straight to us," Murder said as he pushed the send button and began to patiently wait for Carter to take the bait. "Now, we just sit back and wait," he said just before he got up and walked over to Miamor. He stood over her and bent down to kiss her on her forehead. "I'm taking you back home, Miamor. Everything's going to be all right," he whispered in her ear as she slept comfortably. "I love you." Murder had never said that to anyone, besides Miamor. He had never trusted anyone enough to extend something so great, but as he looked down at her, he knew that he meant every word.

"I love you too Carter," Miamor whispered back, while still in her sleep. It was obvious that Murder was not the man in her dreams. Hearing those words were like daggers through his heart, but he understood. He was just ready to end The Cartel and move Miamor back to Brooklyn, where she belonged.

Carter watched as the movers moved all of the expensive décor and statues from the Diamond

Estate. The immaculate mansion didn't even look the same now that it was half empty. Carter's Phoenix venture was all in place. His partners were just waiting on his arrival to get the ball rolling. The Cartel was about to go legit and leave the entire street business behind. Carter possessed all of the business savvy his father once had, but never knew how much he was like him. He felt his BlackBerry vibrate and quickly pulled it off of his waist and looked at it. It was a text from Miamor, asking him to meet her somewhere so they could make things right between them. He quickly dismissed it and shook his head. He missed her dearly, but he hated her at the same time. She had betrayed him to the fullest extent, and in the process she broke his heart, making him feel like a fool. He knew that he should have killed her on behalf of The Cartel, but he could not pull the trigger. There was a small part in him that still loved her, even though she was responsible for the fall of his family. *Why can't I let her go?* Carter asked himself as he slowly paced the room with his hands behind his back. The clicking sounds of his Mauri gators echoed throughout the house as he thought deeply about Miamor. Zyir walked in, interrupting his thoughts. "I'm all packed up and ready to leave this mu'fucka for good," he said and his Jordan sneaks scuffed the marble floor. "Phoenix is a good look," he said as he approached Carter and slapped hands while embracing him. "About that," Carter said as he stepped back. "I want you to fall back for a month or two. Go back to Flint and I'll send for you," he said as he looked into Zyir's eyes.

"Wha . . . What? Why you want me to go back home, Carter?" Zyir asked, totally confused about Carter's sudden change of heart.

"Zyir, it's not what you're thinking. I am doing this to protect you. You are the only one that I fully trust on this earth. Mecca's my brother, but his head isn't always in the right place. He's impulsive, while you are a thinker. You plan every move before you make it. You are like a little brother to me, and I just want you to be safe. I want to check out the new turf first, and then I'll send for you. I need you out of harm's way for a while, just in case something happens to me. If that day comes, you will know what to do. I've already made arrangements just in case you have to step into my shoes," Carter said, thinking two steps ahead.

"I don't get it, fam," Zyir said with a confused look on his face.

"I'm taking a lot of money up there to get washed, feel me? I don't know if I am dealing with undercover agents or what. If anything goes down, I want you to be safe and I want to leave my business in the hands of someone I trust. You all I got left, Zy," Carter said as he put his hand on the back of Zyir's neck. Carter knew that Zyir would not like the news, but it was something that he had to do. Zyir was exactly like him. He had the same swagger, same morals, and same thought process as he did. Carter practically built Zyir from the ground up to be a real nigga. He would never be able to forgive himself if Zyir got caught up in some bullshit on his account. Carter kissed the top of Zyir's head and pulled him close. That was his li'l man, and he had much love for him. He knew that Zyir was a boss in the making, but that was not the path he wanted for him. He had big plans for his little man that would introduce him to an entirely new world . . . the business world. All Zyir had to do was be patient. "Just trust me, family. Just trust me," Carter said as he released Zyir.

Zyir felt like his world had come crashing down. To not be with Carter was like taking his other half. Carter was his nigga, his father figure, and his only family. He wanted to protest, but Carter had yet to tell him anything wrong, so he nodded his head in agreement. "Okay," he answered in reluctant agreement.

"Cool. I got your plane tickets on the table in there. Your stuff will be sent to you when you get up there. You got your paper up, right?" Carter asked, referring to Zyir's cash.

"No doubt," Zyir confirmed as he thought about the half million dollars he had stashed away in a foreign account. The proceeds from the Miami drug game had done him lovely, and he had enough to be comfortable at that point. He walked into the room to retrieve his one-way ticket to the murder capital of Flint, Michigan. He knew something was wrong with Carter, but could not place his finger on it. In Zyir's eyes it was as if Carter was telling him good bye.

Carter's flight was scheduled for that next morning, and he was ready to leave everything behind. No matter what he did, he couldn't get his mind off of Miamor. He felt his phone buzz again and he looked at the screen. It was Miamor again. "Just leave me alone, Mia! You're killing me!" he said in a low whisper as he dismissed the text.

Zyir returned back to the front with his plane ticket in his hand. He saw the look in Carter's eyes, and there was no mistaking that something was wrong.

The Final Chapter

The Cartel

Carter, please respond. I miss you. I know you're upset, but I need to see you. Love Always, Miamor.

Young Carter read the words twice before deleting the message, just as he had done all the others. It had been seven days since he'd put Miamor out of his hotel room, and she was constantly on his mind. Every message she sent reminded him of what they both had lost. He hoped the relocation would help give him a fresh start.

The Cartel no longer ran Miami. They were out of the drug business and moving on to new heights in a new environment. All of the death, destruction, and deception would be left behind. Miamor would be left behind. He wished that things could be different, but the truth of the matter was she was untrustworthy. He had done her one last favor by keeping Mecca off of her ass. He felt that he owed her that much. Although she had lied to him, everything that he had told her was the truth. He had indeed fallen in love with her, and because of that, he allowed her to live. Now he could skip town and forget that he ever knew her.

The sound of a door opening and closing indicated Mecca's arrival. He walked into the house. His long hair was pulled back into a ponytail, and he wore a sad expression on his face. Carter had never seen Mecca so humble and serene.

Melancholy filled the room as Mecca looked around at the nearly empty mansion. "I came up in this house," he said. "I watched Poppa run his meetings out of this house. Me, Breeze and Money used to play in that backyard." Mecca's eyes had tears in them as he recalled the fond memories of his family, but he let none fall and kept his head held high, just as his father had taught him to do. He wished that he could rewind the clock to happier times, but nothing could erase the hollow feeling he felt. "I'm the last one standing."

Carter didn't respond. He had never known the infamous man who had fathered him, but he respected him all the same. He had grown to love Taryn as much as his own mother, and the deaths of his siblings had destroyed him because he had been robbed of his time with his newfound family.

"It doesn't feel right leaving all this behind," Mecca stated.

"We have to," Carter stated. He extended his hand to Mecca, and they embraced briefly. Carter picked up his Louis luggage, and they both headed toward the door. All of the other contents of the house had already been shipped to Arizona. A new house would be set up and waiting when they arrived.

"Where is Zyir?" Mecca asked.

"He has a couple stops to make, but he'll be flying back to Flint tonight. The arrangements are already made for him," Carter explained.

Carter's BlackBerry rang out loud, and he saw that Miamor had text him again.

Carter, if you ever really loved me, please text me back. I'm sorry for everything. I don't want to lose you.

Mecca watched Carter as he typed into his phone. *I know this mu'fucka ain't still in contact with that bitch,* he thought. Mecca had a gut feeling that Carter was responding to Miamor, and although he had given his word to Carter that he wouldn't touch her, he had lied. That was an itch that he was determined to scratch. He just couldn't let his hatred for her go. He had a score to settle, and he had a good feeling that he was going to get a chance to do it before he left Miami. His brother was going to lead him right to her.

Sorry's not enough. I'm leaving town tonight. Good luck with your life, ma, Carter typed back.

Within seconds, his phone was going off again with another message from Miamor.

Carter, please do not leave me like this. At least give me a chance to say good-bye. Meet with me, Carter.

Please. I won't take up too much of your time. I just want to see you.

"What's up, fam?" Mecca inquired, trying to sound casual.

Carter looked up at him. "Oh, ain't shit. Just a little something I forgot to take care of. What time does the private jet take off?"

"Six o'clock," Mecca replied.

Carter looked at his watch. It was only three p.m. That left him with three hours to spare. He thought about never seeing Miamor again, and his stomach turned over. She was right. They did need to see each other face to face before he left. They needed closure.

There's a warehouse in Opa-locka on Twenty-seventh Ave. Meet me there in an hour.

Carter instructed Mecca to meet him at the landing strip, and the two parted ways.

"It's about fucking time!" Robyn yelled out as she flipped Miamor's Sidekick closed. She looked at Aries and Murder. "He responded. He thinks he's meeting her in Opa-locka in an hour."

Murder was about to put his game down like only he could do, and a devilish leer spread across his face. He went into the closet and put on black gloves and grabbed a black .45. He tucked it into his waistline.

"We should come with chu," Aries stated as she stood.

Murder shook his head. "Aries, you stay here with Miamor. Robyn, you come with me. I'ma personally rock this nigga to sleep. When Miamor comes out of the shower, get her ready to go. Pack up all our shit and wipe the room down. We I get back, we're out," he explained.

Miamor closed her eyes as the stream of shower water licked her wounds. She was still not at full health, but was grateful for the little bit of strength that was returning to her limbs. *At least I can stand up and walk around without passing out,* she thought as she washed her body. A part of her was happy to be getting out of Miami. She had too many bad memories here. It was where her sister had been killed, where she had almost been killed, and where she had lost the man she loved. *Fuck Miami!* she thought bitterly. She was trying to rebuild her callous attitude. Being tough had stopped her from being hurt in the past. She had built walls around herself that only Carter had been able to scale. *Forget about him. He doesn't want you. It's over,* she said to herself.

She got out of the shower and wrapped a towel around her body. Green bruises covered her everywhere, but her body was healing and she was grateful for that. If only her heart would heal as well.

She walked out into the room and saw Aries packing up their things. "What's going on?" she asked.

"Nothing, Mia. Get dressed. When Murder and Robyn come back, we're leaving," Aries stated.

"For New York?" Miamor asked.

"Yeah."

"Tonight?"

"Yeah, Mia, we are leaving tonight," Aries said as she looked on in sympathy. She knew that Miamor was mourning over losing Carter.

When all of their bags were by the door, Aries turned and said, "Me will go fill up the tank at the station on the corner. Mia, chu need anything while I'm out?"

Miamor shook her head no as she stepped into a pair of Robyn's Juicy Couture sweat pants and put on a wife beater and sneakers. "Nah, go ahead. I'm good."

Aries shrugged. "All right. Me will be right back. By the time they get back, we'll be ready to dip."

Aries left out, and Miamor locked the door behind her. She lay down on the bed and closed her eyes, when her phone began to ring. She walked over to the dresser where her phone lay. She hadn't checked it since she had been there. She had forgotten that she even had it. The name "Carter Jones" appeared on her screen, and butterflies instantly appeared in her stomach. She flipped open her PDA and saw that she had an unread text message:

I'm on my way

She frowned when she read the message. "On your way where?" she asked aloud. Miamor searched the outbox of her phone, and her eyes widened in shock. *I didn't send these,* she thought as she read through every one. *They are going to set him up! Carter's going to walk right into a trap!* She put her hands over her mouth and speed dialed his number. Her anxious heart felt as if it would explode. She tapped her fingers impatiently against the desk as the phone rang in her ear. The voice mail popped on and she hung up to dial him again.

"Pick up the phone!" she urged nervously, knowing that Carter's life rested in her hands. *If Carter arrives at that warehouse, he's dead,* she thought. It wasn't that she thought Carter was a punk, but she knew Murder would expire Carter on sight. When she received his voice mail again, she screamed in frustration. "Answer the fucking phone!" She tried to reach him once more, but to no avail. Either he wasn't taking her calls, or Murder's job was already complete.

She looked to see what time he had texted her last. *I still have a half an hour*, she thought. She was so overwhelmed that she wanted to cry, but now was not the time for her to bitch up. *I have to get to him,* she thought. *I'm the only person who can stop Murder. I'm the only person who he won't kill.* It had been a long time since she had prayed, or since she had even believed in God, but for this, she raised her head to the sky and closed her eyes. *Please don't let Carter die. I need him.*

She paced back and forth until finally Aries came back. Aries instantly recognized the fire in Miamor's eyes. Miamor tossed the phone at Aries.

"How could you do this?" Miamor asked.

The look on Aries' face established her guilt, but she responded, "We've done this a thousand times."

"I love him!" Miamor yelled. "This time is different!" She took a deep breath, not wanting to overexert herself. She could feel the room start to spin. "Give me the keys," she demanded.

Aries hesitated, but then handed them over without contest. She removed a chrome .45 from her waistline and passed it to Miamor as well.

Miamor brushed past her, and just before she exited the room, Aries called her name. "Mia!"

Miamor turned around and stared at her friend. "I'm sorry."

Miamor didn't respond. She knew that if something happened to Carter, that her relationship with her girls would never be the same. She stormed out of the room, hopped into the rental car and sped off recklessly, praying that she was able to stop the madness before it was too late.

Carter pulled up to the vacant warehouse. It was one of the many stash spots that he had used to store guns and drugs. He sat in the car for a few minutes, trying to gain his composure. *No matter what she says, it's over. I can't trust her,* he told himself. He knew that once he saw her face, his emotions would try and override his intellect. He could not allow that to happen. A beautiful woman had been the downfall of many men. He refused to allow Miamor to lead him to a premature demise. She had showed shade. There was larceny in her heart, and because of that, he had to make a clean break. He exited his vehicle and activated his car alarm, then proceeded into the building. He stopped walking in mid-step and turned around to return to his car. He popped the trunk and hit a button that caused the floor of the trunk to slide back, revealing an arsenal of weapons. He had to remember that he was no longer dealing with the woman he loved. He was dealing with a Murder Mama, and although he did not truly believe that Miamor would harm him, he was not about to walk in unstrapped and chance it. After Miamor's confession, he had done his research on the Murder Mamas, and found out they were more treacherous than he could have imagined. Their work was exquisite, precise, and professional. Carter couldn't imagine Miamor doing some of the jobs that he had heard she had pulled off, and a part of him was intrigued by the mystique of it all. The other part of him was enraged, because she had been hired to take down his family, including him. That put them at odds in a territory where love couldn't exist. He had gone over all the possibilities in his head. There was no way under any circumstances that he would ever be with her.

"He's here," Robyn whispered down to Murder from the second floor. She had a perfect view of the parking lot, and from where she stood, she could easily shoot anything moving on the floor below. She would let Murder handle his business, but if things went awry, she would kill Carter. Robyn watched Carter walk up to the building, then all of the sudden he disappeared. Murder waited behind the front entrance to sneak him from behind. After five minutes passed, Carter still hadn't walked through the door. "Yo, what the fuck the nigga doing?" Murder asked, trying to keep his voice low so that his presence wouldn't be known in the warehouse. "I don't know. I can't see him. He walked right up to the front door, then I lost sight—" Robyn stopped speaking abruptly when she felt the cold kiss of death. Carter was standing behind her with his pistol to her neck. He wasn't a fool, and he didn't run the largest drug operation in Florida for nothing. He didn't trust Miamor, and he was glad he had followed his gut instincts and entered the building through the secret entrance on the side of the building. Carter peered over the ledge to see what he was going up against. He couldn't believe that Miamor had tried to set him up. He could see Murder waiting for him, lurking with his gun already aimed, and he realized that if he had walked through the front door, he would have been shot at point-blank range.

"Murder?" Robyn called out loudly as she struggled against Carter.

Murder looked up to where Robyn hid and saw Carter walk out of the shadows with his gun drawn. Carter had an advantage over him. From where he stood, he could have easily shot him.

"Fuck is you?" Carter asked as he began to descend the steps, with Robyn in a chokehold. He surveyed the room looking for Miamor.

Murder smirked and aimed his gun at Carter.

"I wouldn't do that if I was you. Unless you want me to splatter this bitch's brains all over the floor," Carter threatened.

Murder laughed as if Carter had told a joke, and then without hesitation, he turned his gun toward Robyn.

Boom!

With a marksman's aim, Murder hit Robyn with a hollow tip in the center of her forehead. She folded in Carter's arms, then dropped lifelessly to the concrete floor. She never saw her end coming.

Carter glanced down at Robyn's dead body in disbelief, and in that split second Murder capitalized on the opportunity.

Boom!

Murder let off a shot, hitting Carter in the leg, causing him to drop his gun. Carter didn't even have time to react as he grabbed his leg in pain. "Aghh!" he screamed as a burning flash of heat terrorized him as a bullet ripped through his leg.

Murder wanted to kill Carter slowly. He hated the fact that Miamor had fallen for another man, and he was going to enjoy snuffing his lights out.

Miamor hit 100 mph as she drove and ran through red lights, frantically trying to make it in time. When she was four blocks away, a traffic jam slowed her car down to a crawl. "Damn it!" she yelled as she hit the steering wheel in frustration. "I can't wait this out! He'll die if don't get there!" she whispered urgently. An emotional lump formed in her throat. *Calm down, Miamor,* she told herself. *You can do this . . . you have to do this if you want to save the man you love.*

She grabbed the gun off of the passenger seat and pulled the car over to get out. She could see the tall warehouse about a quarter mile up the street. *I have to run,* she thought wearily. She was doubtful that she could, because she could barely stand on her feet for too long without feeling weak. She knew that her body wasn't ready for what she was about to put it through, but she had no choice. Carter was worth the pain.

Miamor took off running full speed, ignoring the ache of her limbs and the excruciating beat of her heart as she pushed her body to the limit. Her broken ribs screamed in protest with every step that she took. Each time her feet pounded the pavement, she felt as if she would pass out. Her lungs burned, but she refused to stop. "Aghh!" she screamed as she continued on.

No longer able to endure the pain, she stopped and placed her hands on her knees to balance herself. She gulped in air as if she was suffocating, and could no longer stop the tears from coming. "I can't do this!" she whispered. "Murder's going to kill him!"

Carter grabbed his piece off of his ankle holster, and returned fire, sending bullets sailing past Murder's head, and then stood to his feet. "Fuck!" he grimaced as blood soaked through his Evisu jeans. Murder took cover behind a stack of steel barrels and spit bullets until his clip was empty. He immediately put a fresh clip in his gun and ducked for cover, his brief pause giving Carter the chance to gain a slight advantage.

"Fuck you hiding for, you bitch-ass nigga?" Carter screamed as he fired more shots.

Murder couldn't get a shot off. Every time he rounded the corner of the barrels, Carter popped off. He was relentless with his weapons, and he wasn't going to stop until Murder stopped breathing.

Damn! This nigga shooting like his clip don't expire, Murder thought in irritation as he waited for Carter to run out of ammunition. What he didn't know was that Young Carter stayed strapped. He had one in his waistline, one on his ankle, and two in a shoulder holster, so the bullets would be coming for days.

Carter stopped firing and waited, so that Murder would think he had run out of bullets. But as soon as Murder jumped on the opportunity, Carter came up blasting, hitting Murder in the shoulder. The power from the .9mm blew him back, almost knocking him off his feet.

"Aghh! Fuck!" Murder shouted. He was livid. In all the years he had been pulling jobs, he had never been hit. The pain radiated through his shoulder and traveled down his entire body as sweat dripped from his forehead.

Murder stepped from behind the barrels and faced his adversary. Both men extended their guns, standing within five feet of each other, and looking down the barrel of one another's guns. The malice in their eyes displayed their hatred for one another. Carter and Murder wrapped their fingers around their triggers at the same time. They were both prepared to go out in a blaze of glory.

Miamor staggered up to the front door of the warehouse. Her body was so beat up that she practically collapsed into the entrance from fatigue. "Murder, no!" she screamed when she saw the two men that she loved preparing to kill each other. She pulled her gun and pointed it in their direction.

"You sent this nigga here to kill me!" Carter yelled, never taking his eyes off of Murder.

"No! Just please, stop!" she pleaded. "Murder . . . Carter don't do this!"

Miamor's voice fell on deaf ears, because both Murder and Carter kept their weapons locked and loaded.

Miamor let off a shot in the air to get their attention, and then aimed her gun at them.

"Shoot this nigga, Miamor!" Murder ordered. "*He* did this to you. Kill him, Miamor!"

Miamor turned her gun toward Carter, tears in her eyes. Their eyes met. No words needed to be spoken between them for her to know that she couldn't pull the trigger. She sobbed uncontrollably as she changed her mind and turned the gun toward Murder.

"Miamor," Murder uttered, disappointment and hurt in his tone.

Miamor shifted her gun back and forth indecisively. *Who do I choose?* "I can't choose!" she said aloud.

Click-clack!

They heard the sounds of a fourth gun being cocked back. They looked around in confusion, wondering where it was coming from. It wasn't until Miamor turned her head that she saw Mecca Diamond, but by then it was too late.

Boom!

Mecca sent a bullet crashing through Miamor's skull, finally winning the game of life and death they were playing.

"Nooo!" Carter and Murder screamed as they watched in horror as Miamor's body dropped to the ground, and Mecca stepped out of the shadows with a smoking gun in his hand. On instinct, both men loaded Mecca up with bullets.

Mecca's body jerked, and he tried to squeeze off a few crazed shots before the bullets from Murder and Carter's guns robbed him of his life. He went out with a smile, because he had finally gotten his revenge. Now he was going to reunite with the rest of the Diamond dynasty.

Carter rushed to Miamor's side and held her in his arms. The crimson hole in her temple let him know that she was long gone, but he cradled her anyway, and cried as he kissed the top of her head. He was in shock and hysterical. All of the beef that he had been through, and all of the material things that he had gained seemed worthless to him now as he sat in a puddle of Miamor's blood. Her death had broken him down to his weakest state.

Murder fell to his knees and put his hands on the top of his head. His heart was broken and in complete anguish as tears also fell down his face. He pointed his gun at Carter. "You did this to her!" Murder screamed. He wanted to end Carter, but it would not bring Miamor back. Murder lowered his weapon and hit the floor with his bare hands as he cried and mourned over Miamor.

Carter didn't focus on anything but the woman in his arms. He tuned everything else out as he spoke in Miamor's ear. "I'm so sorry, ma! I love you, Miamor! Wake up for me, ma! You got to wake up!" Carter cried. "Wake up, ma . . . wake up! Wake up!"

"Wake up, bitch!" Miamor gasped and sucked in air as her eyes shot open and she looked around in confusion. Her vision was blurry, but she could see that her arms were still bound, and Fabian loomed over her, swinging the deadly chain in his hands. "It's about time you woke up, bitch! I thought you had died on me for a minute," he said with a devious smile. "You passed out, but don't worry, I'ma make sure the next time you black out it'll be for good." "Carter . . . Murder?" she mumbled frantically as she looked around the basement that she was trapped in. The hope that had filled her slowly fizzled away. *I passed out. None of it was real,* she thought as tears came to her eyes. *I'm dying. I just saw my entire life flash before my eyes. It was all a dream. I'm right back where I started . . . right back at the beginning. None of it ever really happened. Carter, Murder, Mecca, Breeze . . . I made it all up in my head.* It was at that moment that Miamor realized that she was not invincible. This was not a dream, and the lifestyle that she had lived was finally catching up to her. Her karma had come full circle. *I'm going to die down here,* she admitted to herself.

Miamor was truly terrified, and she began to weep as she realized there was no avoiding her fate. "It was all a dream!" she whispered in disbelief as she cried desperately. The mind is a powerful tool. It's the most powerful weapon that a human possesses, and when Miamor's body could no longer endure the physical pain, her mind had temporarily taken her to a different time and place . . . to a place of relief. But now that she was awake, her circumstance was still the same.

The putrid smell of human waste mixed with blood filled the air. This was truly hell on earth, and her torture had just begun. It wouldn't end until Fabian said so, and he had a whole lot planned for her before putting her out of her misery.

Her eyes widened as Fabian lifted the chain and brought it down across her naked body. "Aghhh!" Miamor screamed in agonizing pain. Just when she thought it was all over, the torture had just begun.

The entire story you just read was all a figment of Miamor's imagination. Not until you open the pages of The Cartel 3 *will you figure out her fate.*

The Cartel 3, OUT NOW!

ORDER FORM
URBAN BOOKS, LLC
97 N18th Street
Wyandanch, NY 11798

Name (please print):_____

Address:_____

City/State:_____

Zip:_____

QTY	TITLES	PRICE
	16 On The Block	$14.95
	A Girl From Flint	$14.95
	A Pimp's Life	$14.95
	Baltimore Chronicles	$14.95
	Baltimore Chronicles 2	$14.95
	Betrayal	$14.95
	Black Diamond	$14.95

Shipping and handling-add $3.50 for 1st book, then $1.75 for each additional book.
Please send a check payable to:
Urban Books, LLC
Please allow 4-6 weeks for delivery

ORDER FORM
URBAN BOOKS, LLC
97 N18th Street
Wyandanch, NY 11798

Name (please print):_____

Address:_____

City/State:_____

Zip:_____

QTY	TITLES	PRICE
	Black Diamond 2	$14.95
	Black Friday	$14.95
	Both Sides Of The Fence	$14.95
	Both Sides Of The Fence 2	$14.95
	California Connection	$14.95
	California Connection 2	$14.95

Shipping and handling-add $3.50 for 1st book, then $1.75 for each additional book.
Please send a check payable to:
Urban Books, LLC
Please allow 4-6 weeks for delivery

ORDER FORM
URBAN BOOKS, LLC
97 N18th Street
Wyandanch, NY 11798

Name (please print):_____

Address:_____

City/State:_____

Zip:_____

QTY	TITLES	PRICE
	Cheesecake And Teardrops	$14.95
	Congratulations	$14.95
	Crazy In Love	$14.95
	Cyber Case	$14.95
	Denim Diaries	$14.95
	Diary Of A Mad First Lady	$14.95
	Diary Of A Stalker	$14.95

Shipping and handling-add $3.50 for 1st book, then $1.75 for each additional book.
Please send a check payable to:
Urban Books, LLC
Please allow 4-6 weeks for delivery